CW01567101

ROSES ARE RED
VIOLETS KILL YOU

AN ALBERTUS OAK MYSTERY

BEN DARK

FOLDING HOUSE

First published 2020 by Folding House

This edition first published 2020 by Folding House

ISBN: 978-1-913570-00-2

FOLDING HOUSE

1

----

agic is funny stuff. The few who believe tend to picture it drifting about like oxygen. But that's not right at all. Magic doesn't float — it pools and drips. It's thick, like honey spilled on the breakfast table. It obeys laws more esoteric than gravity, oozing and coagulating, seeping into forgotten corners, forming invisible ponds and marshlands of supernatural energy.

In most places magic is as thin as rain on the pavement. Some towns have none at all; they have other things, like estate agents and commuter trains. Others are inundated by deep, sticky, lakes of the stuff. My village of Wittleshin is at the bottom of one such lake. We take it in on each breath and with each bite. We sleep under a soft, fat supernatural duvet. We are out of our depth, drowning in magic.

Something here draws the paranormal. Maybe it's the ley lines that cross under the green, or the white horse carved into the hill above us. Things are strange, and it isn't just energy, it's the residents. We have known the landlord of the local pub change into a dog at last orders and we have all, once or twice, fallen in love with a shadow. Ours is a place of mystery. We've had a year last thirteen months, all of them May and more people have climbed out of the old wishing well than have ever fallen in.

Most people in the village have no idea about the mythical creatures in their midst. We tend be wary around newcomers, letting some magic seep into them before we reveal anything about our true natures.

My new boss was not allowing me that opportunity.

"You want me to pull up *all* the roses?"

We were standing under the spread of a knotted beech tree. Beyond its circle of shade sun heated the gardens. The lawns and meadows thrummed with insect song and up high the larks trilled.

I had a mug of tea in my hand and a good morning's work under my belt. Until now it had been an almost perfect day.

I had known that there would be changes. Pentdown Hall was under new ownership and one could hardly expect young Miss Lorna Brimtide to want the same plantings and landscaping as her grandfather, but this was a little more than I was ready for. After all, the small stately home at which I was proud to call myself Head Gardener was famous across Southern England for its sweet smelling rose gardens. Was she really suggesting that I yanked out hundreds of years' worth of understated floral achievement?

"The public rather like roses," I said, lamely.

"Well I don't. They are so... provincial."

I wondered just where she thought she was if not in the provinces. The tiny village of Wittleshin was long on cows and wheat fields and short on metropolitan chic.

"What would you prefer in their place?" I asked.

Over many years spent gardening I have found that most people know the names of very few plants. Ask them what they like and they'll say: 'the yellow ones, you know, with green leaves.' Once Lorna was made aware of her own ignorance she would have more faith in my professional opinion.

"Well, I was thinking maybe giant hogweed." She smiled brightly.

"A more exciting plant than the rose," I conceded. Truth be told, she was right. I loved the exuberant flower spikes of the giant hogweed, the way it held its seeds way up, twice the hight of a man, like an overhead explosion. It was a dramatic plant. A talking point. But it had disadvantages in a garden open to the public.

"You do realise that plant causes horrendous blistering of the skin?" I said. "It's a certified menace."

"Yes. And?"

"And, well... it might not be the best plant to have in a garden with as many visitors as this one. It does put people in hospital."

"Oh poppycock," said Lorna. "If someone can't visit a garden without wandering off into the flowerbeds and getting their skin burned off then they're not the visitor we want at Pentdown Hall. These plants can be our security against the imbecilic."

I nodded and jotted the idea down in my notebook: 'roses out hogweed in, security against the imbecilic.'

"Well, looks like I've got a bit of a job to get started with," I said, hoping to get away before Lorna could come up with another radical suggestion, replacing the lawns with gravel maybe, or turning all the trees upside down.

"Wait a moment Albertus, there were a few more changes. I've been looking at the long border, and to me it seems a little... I don't know... pedestrian?"

That hurt. Insult my intelligence, criticise my appearance, but leave the herbaceous borders out of it. The thick strip of flower bed was my pride and joy. Every year by early summer it was a multi-coloured riot of clashing shades and subtle textures. It had won Wittleshin in Bloom's Best Flower Bed award five years running. Anyone who could call it pedestrian was unhinged.

"I'm not sure I understand," I said, telling myself that there was no use getting angry - Lorna Brimtide knew nothing about gardens and she'd just proved it beyond all reasonable doubt.

"You know, all those delphiniums and lupins and alstroemeria. I know they're pretty, and traditional, and just the ticket for a nice little village like Wittleshin, but really Albertus they are so boring! Everyone's got them. I see them wherever I go. Don't you ever want to create something truly special? We want this border to make people say 'wow!'"

I made another note in the book, pressing the pen down hard enough to send the nib through the paper and onto the page below: *Say wow!* Lorna's casual suggestion that the gardens contained nothing special was a brutal repudiation of my life's work. Something I was unprepared for on such a mild summer's morning.

"Well, if you have the budget we could get more accent plants." I searched my mental index of plants for things that would impress a city girl. "Maybe some foxtail lilies, or some tree echiums, you don't see many of those round here."

"Foxtail lilies, smoxtail lilies! I want something exciting! Something new, something you would never see at the Chelsea Flower Show, something they don't drone about on *Gardeners' Question Time* every week. I was thinking about dog mercury."

'Dog mercury?' It went down in the book, extra emphasis on the question mark. When I agreed to take a stroll around the grounds I had expected Pentdown Hall's new owner to be clueless about plants, but her suggestion wasn't ignorant, just weird. I liked dog mercury, an affable little plant, if slightly poisonous. We'd had some enjoyable conversations over the years, but no one would call it a showstopper.

"Anything else?" I asked with trepidation.

"Yes actually. I was thinking maybe dropwort, hounds tongue, darnall, ragwort, wolfsbane, nightshade, brugmansia, mandrake, hensbane and monkshood."

I stopped writing. Lorna was no dilettante.

She looked at me, her head tilted. "Well Mr Oak, you're the gardener, what do you think?"

I hesitated, part of me was excited, even if it was unadulterated lunacy. Were we on the edge of doing a very bad thing? I felt like a school boy with a snowball in hand and a clear view of the headmaster.

"I'm sure that border would look very interesting, and there wouldn't be anything like it in the rest of the county, the only thing that worries me is that we would be growing enough poisonous plants to kill the whole village fifteen times over," I said.

"Yes, that's the point. Isn't it a wonderful plan? I'm sure it would become quite the attraction. A garden crossed with an adventure park. Who wants to look at boring old hostas when you can dice with death at the hands of the Devil's trumpet?"

"Angel's trumpet," I said. "Brugmansia is Angel's trumpet."

"Angels, devils, what's the difference? This garden will be something to get people talking. A garden of death to bring life to a stuffy old bit of England. We could have a grand opening and serve green cocktails that bubble with dry ice and jet black canapés! That would give all those stuffy villagers something to talk about! And if they start dying - well, we can't be blamed for that."

Lorna Brimtide should not have joked about the villagers of Wittleshin dying — it was something they were all too prone to doing. In my long life I had seen many neighbours killed by improbable catastrophes. There had been the Cheese Crash of 1929 when a wheel of cheddar had broken free on White Horse Hill and demolished four cottages and a motor car. I lost several friends and a hat in the Eel Storms of 1851 and I was still recovering from the visit of Sir Christopher's Fenniwicks Sword Juggling Circus in 1753. I didn't want *a day trip to Pentdown Hall* going down in history as one leading causes of death in the locality. There were too many graves in the churchyard as it was.

Of course I could see things from Lorna's point of view. Her Grandfather, Sir Lionel Brimtide, had been a little traditional in his choice of plants. He had cared more about antiques and esoteric books than the grounds. The planting here was a little boring. Every manor, mansion and miniature castle for a hundred miles probably sported the same vegetation in differing arrangements. But if we were going to make a poison garden, it would be me planting and maintaining the death-dealing landscaping.

Admittedly, my particular gifts gave me an advantage over human gardeners in these situations. My ability to communicate with plant-life meant that I could get most of them to behave, but still, there was no point trying to reason with brugmansia. Angel's trumpet was now extinct in its natural habitat, the high foothills of the Andes Mountains. The scientific consensus blamed the loss of a pollinating moth, but I knew different. The brugmasia was hunted down by the native tribes who grew sick of the psychosis it caused, the druggings it was responsible for and the rogue chieftains who used it to comatose their households prior to live burial. In flower it was a beautiful thing but it was insane and delirious on its own alkaloids. Gardening is largely about harmony and this was a plant that would upset the daisies and traumatise the sweet peas — there was no way I would let it into the grounds of Pentdown Hall.

"And," said Lorna. "I was thinking we needed something special, a real showstopper of a plant. One that no one round here will have ever seen before. A flower we can put front and centre, like the tigers at London Zoo. Something guaranteed to draw the crowds."

"How about a rose? They've always brought in lots of visitors."

"We will have no sarcasm in this garden please. No. I was thinking, maybe... elf violet?"

I stopped taking notes and stared at her. I squinted and winced and contorted my fairly presentable features into those of a mad man. Then I spotted it. A faint purple flame way down in her wide black irises — the tiny spark that suggested there was something different about her.

I don't know why I hadn't noticed it sooner, you don't live as long as I have without developing an instinct for recognising other magical creatures. She had hidden it better than most, maybe years of living in the city encouraged one to be more guarded, but she couldn't obscure it. There was something magical about this woman.

I struggled to place her. Not a vampire, the sun was too strong for her to be out. She wasn't a succubus either, she was beautiful but she didn't have that pin you down and suck the lifeblood out of you sexiness of the succubi. She could have been a member of the were-canon, a were-wolf or were-bear, or maybe even a were-weasel, but if so I wouldn't be able to find out until the next full moon. Perhaps she was an attractive hobgoblin, I had known a few.

"Albertus? Are you okay?"

I had been gazing at her. Looking like the yokel she took me for. I tried to remember what had got me onto the supernatural, but my mind was blank. Could she be an enchantress? Or a neuromancer? A hypo-thaumaturge?

"What were we talking about?" I probed.

"Elf violet," she said.

"Yes, elf violet. You know there is no such plant?"

She looked at me stonily.

"It's a myth, just folklore." I continued. "What about something like a Wollemi pine? No one around here will have seen one before because everyone thought they were extinct until a few decades ago. They can grow to be pretty spectacular, given the right climatic conditions. Also, they have the huge advantage of existing."

Was she buying it? The fewer people that knew the truth about elf violet the better. The most potent of medicines and the most deadly of poisons. It was tasteless odourless and invariably fatal. After consuming it victims felt no symptoms until exactly forty-five minutes later when their heart would rupture and they would fall down dead and slightly blue.

Until Lorna mentioned it I thought the plant's elegant flower spikes were only remembered by the tree-folk like me and the Fairies. It struck me that perhaps she was one of the Fae, but no, she was too tall for that, and she didn't look tricksey enough.

"Elf violet exists. I've seen it. What is more I know you grow it here. It's in that patch you think is hidden behind your cottage, next to the raspberries," Lorna said.

"That's not elf violet, that's just a particularly gothic strain of borage. I think you've read too many fairy tales."

But Lorna wouldn't be bamboozled by borage-talk. "Don't lie to me, I know elf violet when I see it. Why should it be a great big secret, Albertus? If you people hadn't been hiding it away for centuries it wouldn't have such a bad reputation."

"Us people? You mean gardeners?"

"No Albertus, I don't. You know what I mean. Poisons

are very useful in medical research. Think of the lives that could have been saved if elf violet had been given to the scientific community for proper study."

"Think of the lives that could have been saved, you say? Think of all the lives that would have been lost! I mean, that would have been lost if such a thing existed. Which it categorically doesn't." You'd think with over 400 years to practice I'd be better at lying. It's the wood in me — I'm not very good at deceiving people.

Lorna cackled and I knew the truth. She was a witch. It should have been obvious from the beginning: the confidence in her voice, her exceptional knowledge of plants. This poison garden wouldn't be a tourist attraction; it would be her herbal medicine cabinet — a potion factory.

"You've given yourself away," said Lorna. "You're lying to me. That's sad. I didn't want to get off on a bad foot. First, because we will have to work together, and, second, because I've never met a real dryad before."

She stepped towards me with her eyes narrowed.

"I suppose I've never met one because there just aren't many dryads left nowadays. From what I hear the woods round here used to be full of them. But I suppose it's because most of the trees have been cut down. You dryads have all been turned into bonfires and barn doors. It really is a shame just how prevalent deforestation has become. It must be a worry, never knowing if someone will come along and take an axe to your spirit trunk. I'd hate for something like that to happen on my new estate. Maybe to..." she paused and looked at me like a hawk on a hamster. "...the big ash tree by the lake?"

Something in my face signposted my relief. She

shook her head and carried on talking. "No, no, and no. Not the ash tree. You are too broad to be an ash spirit. In that case I hate to see anything happen to... the yew tree by the gate?"

I said nothing, trying to affect a poker face. If my home tree died then I died. One bargain we dryads made in return for an extraordinary long life was to live in constant fear of high winds and chainsaws. Although I didn't have many enemies I made a point of never giving away which was my spirit tree. I'd had enough cousins turned into dining sets and sawdust.

"No, not the yew, you don't look wise enough."

She scanned the garden for a moment and then her eyes lit up. "The oak! The big oak, that's your home tree! The one down in the bottom meadow. There is no point denying it, I can read it on your face. You'd make an awful card player, Albertus." She clapped her hands.

"And you'd make a fine detective. The clue was in my name though, Albertus Oak. I would hardly be a willow."

"Well, no. Anyway, Mr Oak." Her tone was serious again. "I understand that there are quite a few people interested in buying fields hereabouts. You know how property prices are in a village as desirable as Wittleshin. They want to build housing. It would be accommodation that this community desperately needs, but I'm sure no developers would want an inconvenient old tree slap bang in the middle of their new housing estate, would they?"

I said nothing. My new boss was blackmailing me on her first day, it had taken her grandfather years to get around to it. This, I thought, is what comes of spending too much time in London. That place was one big, city-sized academy for evil, where nice, friendly country folk when to learn how to pick-pocket and jump red lights on their bicycles. The pendulum was swinging towards Lorna Brimtide being a very wicked witch indeed.

"I really do need to work out whether I should sell that field," Lorna continued. "It will require a lot of good hard thought. So while I puzzle out what to do, why don't you go down to your cottage, divide the clump of elf violet that you claim doesn't exist, and bring me a little up here? It might help my decision making if I have a nice plant to look at. How does that sound to you, Albertus?"

"You're a monster," I said.

Lorna smiled. "I think we are going to have the most fun, you and I. The poison garden will be our masterpiece!"

2

B ack in the cottage garden I lifted the elf violet. I drove the blade of my spade into the ground two times on each side and hauled the plant out in a cube of soil, before splitting it with a single chop. One section I popped in a wheelbarrow, making sure not to touch it with my bare hands, the other I firmed back into its hole with the heel of my boot.

I should explain why I was growing such deadly herbaceous perennials. I am not a poisoner. I grew elf violet because it was beautiful and because it was unusual. Like many long term gardeners I have become hooked on esoteric plants. For me the more obscure the better. Growing a shrub or bulb so rare that no one believes in its existence is the end-point of this all-consuming addiction.

"I'm only doing my job," I told myself as I wheeled the deadly cargo towards Pentdown Hall. Late afternoon was fading into evening. Heat and hard thoughts befuddled my brain. After dropping the plant at the kitchen door I decided the only thing for it was to go down the pub for a restorative pint.

Pentdown Hall lay in fading splendour at the end of a long drive lined with pleached limes. Beyond its stone gateposts was a little country lane, high-banked and hedged. As I stepped into it cows with foolish faces peered at me over the hawthorn. From hidden fields came the bleating of sheep. The lane thrummed with insect and bird noise, and in a lower, leafier register that only I could hear, with the slow chatter of the plants.

I walked fast to the village, hoping I could make the mile-and-a-half while meeting no one. It's not that I'm an antisocial person, I just suffer from what I call Gardener's Walk. I cannot pass the most casual of acquaintances without being accosted and drained of expertise. Conversations start with pleasantries, but quickly hints are dropped about yellowing acanthus and mildewed Michaelmas daisies, and then comes the inevitable question, 'I don't suppose you could pop round and have a look?' and before I know it I'm in some back garden holding a cup of tea and a border fork. Normally I'm happy to stop and help my neighbours, but I was reeling from Lorna's threats and I wanted to keep my head down and reach the pub without bother.

Whoever orders the Universe evidently regards my wants as unimportant. I was barely past the first row of thatched cottages when I heard someone calling my name:

"Cooie, Albertus! Bertie, darling, how are you?"

I considered faking deafness, but it wasn't plausible; Felicity Jenkins had a voice that could be heard the next village over.

"Hello Felicity," I said, pretending to have been daydreaming. "I didn't notice you there. How are you today?"

"I'm well, I'm well," she chirruped. "Though I do have one tiny question..."

Mrs Jenkins was one of my more problematic acquaintances. She was recently divorced. A manic blur of blond hair, red lipstick and overly tight blouses. In the old days women like her wouldn't have given me a second glance. A hundred years earlier gardeners had not been fashionable. Back then my work worn clothes and my inability to control my curly hair had spoken of poverty and poor upbringing. Over the decades tastes had changed. Now a semi-wild man had become a more attractive prospect. I had been trying to dodge Felicity's advances even before her husband ran off with their cleaning lady.

"Felicity. What is it this time?" I asked, more briskly than was polite.

"Oh, in a rush are we? I like a man with things to do. Not like that some I could mention, lying around on the sofa like fifteen stone of bacon. Don't worry I won't keep you long. It's those daffodils you planted for me."

"What about them?"

"Well, they've gone."

"It's late June, that's what daffodils do."

Felicity laughed and laid a hand on my arm. "Yes I know that, I'm not that silly. But these ones, they seemed to do it differently, almost like they weren't happy." She gave me a meaningful look. "Perhaps you could come in and take a peek at them. It's a lovely evening and I was just about to open a bottle of wine."

On most other days good manners would have left me powerless to resist. It is not in my nature to let people down, even if their motives are absurdly transparent. But this was not a normal evening. I was in the grip of mental turmoil and physical thirst. A pint of ale and nothing else could cure both. "I'm very sorry Felicity, but I'm late already. Something is waiting for me in the Bull and Firkin."

"Oh, you're going to the pub? I was just about to head down there myself. Hang on a moment, I'll get my purse."

"I thought you were just about to open a bottle of wine?"

"Oh yes, well if you'd prefer wine I can do that, or I can come to the pub. Either. Your choice."

"Well I'm going to the pub. You are more than welcome to come with me. But I'm afraid that I won't be able to talk to you. I have a date."

"Oh, right you are," said Felicity, her face crumpling like she'd taken a swig of sour milk. "Actually, now that I think about it my cousin said she might call later from Australia. I'd better stay in for that."

Lies do not come naturally to me but there was some truth in what I had just said, it was just that my date would come from a beer barrel and not the internet where, according to Lupin, dates came from these days. Still, the hurt on Felicity's face was clear to see. I girded my loins and turned to leave. "If you change your mind you know where I am!" I called over my shoulder as I strode off down the hill. "And I promise I'll pop in about those disappearing daffodils some other time."

I passed the church without further interruption and was in the bosom of the village. If you close your eyes and picture an English rural village you'd do a good enough job in conjuring up Wittleshin, but I'll help you along. There at the end of that row of cottages is the village shop, selling pipe tobacco, lemon drops and newspapers. Next door is the bakers and beyond that the pub. These three make up the capitalist heart of the village and in good years all three have been known to turn a small profit.

Opposite this commercial triad is the pond, home to ducks, moorhens and a thing with tentacles who rises from the stinking mud every fifty years — not this year, or even this decade, you'll be relieved to find out. Next to the pond is a red phone box, naturally, and beyond that the village green. A small stream feeds the pond and an ancient hump-backed bridge crosses it. Like our houses the bridge is built from the honey coloured local stone giving the village a warm look in all but the foulest of weather. It is, in short, a fine place to spend a long lifetime.

I had nearly made it. I was within touching distance of the hanging-basket covered façade of the Bull and Firkin when I was struck down once more by Gardener's Walk.

An earsplitting trill from the doorway of the baker's brought me to a halt. From the shop emerged the unmistakable figure of Mrs Dobson, a full four-foot eleven of indomitable good-deeds and gossip.

"Albertus, just the man I was looking for."

My pint of ale had grown distant, conversations with Mrs Dobson went on for hours.

"Hello Mrs Dobson. Shopping for cakes, were you?" I nodded at the bakery. Some happy wasps had found their way into the window display and were buzzing between the iced buns and the Bakewell tarts.

"Shopping for cakes indeed! I make my own cakes! Have done for sixty years, since I married my Wilfred, just because he's dead doesn't mean I've stopped making his favourites, does it? Victoria sponge every Sunday and maybe a fruit cake of a Friday. Of course my niece says that I shouldn't bother if I'm only going to feed them to the birds, but its tradition, isn't it? And tradition's more important than overfed sparrows all week long, that's what I always say. Of course my niece wouldn't understand that, her daughter, the one who's away at university, she's going to Ibiza for a week. Her mother says they all do it and that it's nothing to worry about, but I've seen the programs on the television. It will be drugs and boys and beats. Yes beats! That's what young people call music you know, except it's not really music, just noise. Anyway it will be nothing but beats all week long, and boys. When I was her age I was already married and let me tell you we had no time for Spanish rave-parties. A long weekend in Bournemouth was what we got, and we were grateful for it. I married young, but everyone did back then, so it wasn't really young, seems one day I was out climbing trees, I used to be good at climbing trees, best of all the Girl Guides, then the next moment I was married with an apron and a family. My niece..."

"Mrs Dobson," I interrupted. "I'm in a rush, what can I do for you?" I hoped that her answer would be to the point, it was incredible the way she talked. I could see why Bella called her The Incredible Gas Bag, she produced enough hot air to power the Bristol Balloon festival.

"I just wanted to ask about how preparations for Wittleshin in Bloom were coming along. Pentdown Hall really is the jewel in our crown. Is the long border looking its best? I only ask because there is some powdery mildew already in my garden, and I know the problems you must have keeping a place like yours watered. My sister, back when she was still alive, she used..."

I cut her off again. "The long border is all anyone will be talking about, I can assure you." I thought it better not to tell her about Lorna's proposed planting scheme of dog mercury and henbane. I wasn't sure her old heart would take it.

"Oh, good. It really adds that hint of class to have a professional involved. My Wilfred said you couldn't trust gardeners. He said they were just hairdressers for plants, and you know what he thought about hairdressers! But I think gardeners are normally very pleasant people, not that you'd want your granddaughter to marry one. Anyway, you'll come along to our summer party next Saturday? I think it's going to be the best one ever, we're having a baking competition, just like they do on the television!"

Mrs Dobson was head of the local Women's Institute, a group of indomitable old ladies who were the undisputed masters of all things knitted, baked, preserved and pickled in the village of Wittleshin. She ran the weekly coffee morning with an iron fist and was constantly on the hunt for new members to replace her ageing population. As a man I was ineligible for conscription, but I was still expected to attend the tea and chat fuelled events.

"I'll try to pop in," I said.

"Oh that is super, Albertus. We're having a flower arranging contest too. Perhaps you could enter. I think I'm in with a fine chance this year. I'm going modern. Very outré. But I don't want to give too much away at this stage of the game, Mrs Treedle has ears everywhere." She looked around suspiciously, her eyes large behind over-sized horn-rimmed spectacles. "It features an ornamental cabbage," she whispered.

I lowered my voice to an conspiratorial volume. "Very good Mrs Dobson. I'm sure no one else stands a chance. If you will excuse me I have a very important appoint-ment." I waved my hand at the Bull and Firkin.

"You're going to the pub? If Arabella is working would you give her this?" She pulled out a thin paper flyer 'COFFEE MORNING MEET AND GREET FOR NEW MEMBERS. ALL WELCOME. FREE CAKE!!!'

I smiled. Mrs Dobson had been trying to get my friend Bella, a part-time barmaid and semi-professional psychic, to join the W.I. for years. The old lady seemed constitutionally unable to take a hint, which was one of the things that made her such a formidable fundraiser. I'd seen her doorstop young Calthrop the carpenter every day for a month until he handed over a quid to buy 'a nice lovely pram' for the new royal baby.

"I will pass it straight over. Now, I really must get on."

Mrs Dobson would not let me get away that easily. "I took a stroll past Pentdown Hall this morning. There was a big removal van turning into the drive. Have you got new tenants? Such a shame about Sir Lionel, I used to be his cleaner you know, I'd hate to think how many hours I spent dusting those old books and funny statues of his. I hope these new tenants..."

"Tenant," I corrected. "Just the one, a young lady. Sir Lionel's granddaughter. In fact, you know how you always say you need new blood for the Institute? Well I think she could be a perfect candidate. She might take a bit of persuading, but she's up there now. Why don't you go back and have a word with her about joining? And Mrs Dobson, don't take no for an answer. She's from London, so she'll probably say she doesn't want to chat. But you don't listen to that. I think she's very lonely. A good natter about the membership benefits of the W.I. is what she wants, even if she doesn't know it yet."

"You are a genius Albertus," she thrilled. "The aristocracy always add a certain *je ne sais quoi* to a cake stand. I'll go home and get some more literature, maybe a bigger brooch, and then I'll head straight up there."

I smiled, watching the gregarious old lady stamp off up the road, her pale blue overcoat buttoned despite the heat of the day. And that is what you get if you try to blackmail Albertus Oak.

THE PUB WAS ALMOST empty and there was no one behind the beer pumps. Skinny Joe Pike, the fattest man in Whittleshin, was at the bar chatting to Steve the Plumber. Both had full glasses and a telltale packet of cheese and onion crisps lay split open between them. Bella could not be far away for snacks and beer did not last long when laid before those two lions. I nodded at the men. Both smiled and sipped in return.

I stood and flicked through a copy of *Shin Digs,* Wittleshin's free magazine. Between listings of village events were classified ads and correspondence from parishioners. There was an angry rant from Mrs Treadle on the subject of rural transport monopolies and an anonymous plea for the return of a pair of trousers, no questions asked. I flicked to my column *The Garden Log* to see how badly the editorial team had mangled my meaning this month. For the June issue I had submitted five-hundred words on my favourite alliums. I closed my eyes and took a deep breath before scanning the page.

The headline was a passable, if obvious 'Know your onions!' The exclamation points no longer made me wince, all *Shin Digs'* headings wore them, and in the magazine's comic sans font they were often the most dignified character. My byline photo was black and white, having been taken in 1896, the main picture was in colour, but blurred to the point of absurdity by the cheap printing process. It was some vast pinkish orb captioned 'Albertus' Purple Sensation.'

"Bella," I called.

There was no reply. I leant over the bar, the hatch that led down to the beer cellar was open but I could hear no noises from the depths.

"Bella!"

"She might be helping Lupin with the food," said Skinny Joe Pike.

I left *Shin Digs* and followed the clattering of pans, the delicious smells and the unholy caterwauling through the swing doors into the kitchen. At the heart of the ruckus was Lupin the werewolf chef, though of course he was in human form at that moment. True wolves are poor cooks. Fear of fire leaves them reliant on cold flesh, but Lupin was in his two legged state and there were flames everywhere. Even without a full moon Lupin is a hairy man, which I think accounted for the howling noise that filled the kitchen, he appeared to have singed all the fuzz from his forearms on a pan that blazed out of control on the stovetop. There was debris all around and what looked like *spaghetti alle vongole* up the walls.

"Productive day Lupin?" I asked, ignoring the mess. Lupin cooked like a convict smashing up his prison cell. The lightest of sautéing engendered loud crashes and dented pans, egg whisking came with violent explosions of yolk and hurled shell. He wielded his rolling pin like a club and his potato-masher like a conductor's baton. If cleanliness is next to godliness he was Satanic, but the devil has all the best flavours and Lupin always emerged from the wreckage with the most delicious dishes. He had once explained to me that food seemed to speak to him the same way a herbaceous border did to me 'a little more salt Lupin, sprinkle me and taste heaven' a bouill-abaisse would whisper, 'a bit of coco powder, just a pinch' his cauliflower risotto had once incongruously suggested, leading to a dinner that had famously made Steve the Plumber cry tears of joy.

'Productive?' The werewolf let out a stream of curses, before extinguishing the pan and calming down. "Here," he said. "Try this."

He gave me a spoonful of golden liquid, the contents of one of the few pans that was neither the wrong way up or on fire. I closed my eyes and sipped the hot broth. It was liquid bliss, somehow rich and sharp at the same time, and infinitely warming. There was a lot of magic pooled around Wittleshin but I sometimes thought we found the most potent in the kitchen of the Bull and Firkin.

"Delicious. What is it?"

"Trade secret I'm afraid," said Lupin with a deep and delighted chuckle, the agonies of preparation forgotten under the joy it always brought him to have his food praised.

"Well I'm sure I'll find out when I see it on the menu. Have you seen Bella?"

"Bella?"

"You know that girl who was always around when you were young? The one who sleeps in the room next to yours? Bella? Your sister?"

Lupin was staring down at his soupy reflection. "No," he said distractedly. "She's probably behind the bar."

"Well I'm going through to have a pint, I need it after the day I've had. Come and join me when you're ready." I left the chef to his kitchen and the dish that was in that moment more important to him than me and my problems with Lorna Brimtide could ever be.

I MADE my way back to the ancient bar and leant my elbow on its smooth surface, rubbed to a shine by the calloused palms of generations past. Guidebooks described the Bull and Firkin as '*A rambling sixteenth century Inn*' but in reality no one knew quite how old it was. At points in its five hundred plus years of history parts had been added, extended, burnt down and rebuilt so it was hard to tell which of its wonky bars and corridors were Tudor, Elizabethan or Georgian. Above the pub Bella and Lupin lived along with a series of bed and breakfasting guests.

"Hello!" I shouted. "Bella? Anybody around?"

"Hello Bertie," a cheerful voice came from the beer cellar. "Bit early for you isn't it?"

"Not after the day I've had," I said. "Have you been down there long? I was calling for you a minute ago."

"Oh right! I think there's an acoustic dead spot down here, listen to this." A strange shamanic humming came up from the hatch. After a moment it cut out, restarting a few seconds later. "See," said Bella. "Down by the peanuts the sound just goes."

"Goes where?"

"Stumped if I know. Though if I'm silent down here I can sometimes hear someone doing the washing up and listening to *The Archers*. It probably goes into that person's house, where ever that is."

"Right. Is this do with one of your...?"

Bella laughed. "I don't think so. But you know how my things are, so probably." Neither of us said the word spell. Skinny Joe Pike and Steve the Plumber were non-magical residents, though they had both been in the village long enough to develop supernatural traits. It was hard to tell as most arcane powers are utterly pointless and easily mistaken for the effects of too many beers. Either way, it was better that they didn't know their barmaid was unironically into pentagrams.

"Are you going to be down there long? I'm very thirsty." I said.

"I'm just checking the ropes and padlocks. That time of the month. I won't be a second, but feel free to go behind the bar and pour yourself a pint."

The time of the month was the full moon, due in all its rotund glory in a few days' time. Although Bella could control her transformed brother using a silver boson's whistle and a drugged rump steak, they took the precaution of tying Lupin up during the twenty-four hours of his metamorphosis. The last time he had gotten loose he had broken into Mr Fairchild's bakery next door and eaten every cake in the place like a very bad dog indeed.

Bella finally emerged from the cellar with a broad grin. She was the world's most cheerful goth but she still stuck to the regulation uniform, claiming that the black clothes and nail varnish she wore was good for her side business as a psychic, even if they clashed with her bright, overpowering laugh.

"Mrs Dobson told me to give you this," I said.

She grimaced at the coffee morning invitation, screwed it up and threw it in the bin.

"How is The Gas-Bag In-Chief?"

"Oh, you know. Her niece's daughter is going to Ibiza, modern music is just noise. The usual."

Bella nodded along, she had received more distracted monologues from Mrs Dodson than I had. "I really don't know why she wants me to join the Women's Institute so badly. I can't bake, I can't make jam and I certainly can't knit. I'd be a liability."

"Fresh blood," I said, "She wants to bleed you."

Bella laughed. "What's all this about a bad day then? I'm sure it can't have been nearly as awful as mine." She leant her elbows on the bar and puffed out her cheeks.

"Yours first," I said. "Then we'll do mine and I'll win and you must give me some sympathy for once. So, what happened?"

"Well you know that date I was supposed to have today? With that guy who was down here for business?"

I winced. Bella did not mix well with online dating. She was blessed, or maybe cursed, with visions of the future, but they weren't always very accurate. Despite her prognostic gifts she invariably picked the most unsuitable men to meet with.

"Well last night I thought I'd do some research, you know into the future, to see how it would all go. So I got out the old crystal ball, and Bertie, let me tell you it was perfect. He was tall, dark and handsome, we had the most amazing meal and then he whisked me off to London in his sports car. I thought I'd found the one. The crystal ball showed a vision of us years later, living with a black cat in a white-walled house in Marrakesh. We both had thick, gorgeous silver hair and laughter lines and we were still so in love."

"And it didn't turn out like that?"

"No it did not! The picture on his profile was a fake. He was short, fat and what hair he had left was grey. The future lied to me again!"

"Well you can't judge a book by its cover, Bella."

"I know. So I thought I'd give him a chance, but when I mentioned holding hands in Marrakesh he went off on a huge rant. He said 'no chance of that luv,' because he'd never take his hands out of his pockets, not with Moroccans around. He thought they'd steal his wristwatch, which was cheap and horrible, by the way. The man was a racist!"

"Oh dear. So what happened?"

"Well, Lupin had cooked us the most amazing late lunch, so we ate it, mostly in silence apart from when he went on about his boring old job, and then he said he had business to attend to and disappeared. Even the ugly racists are rejecting me. I'm going to be single for ever, Bertie."

I grasped Bella's shoulders. "You are a beautiful and talented woman Arabella Lestrade, the men of the world do not know what they are missing. Now if it's not too much bother, I'll have a pint of Wizards Ruin."

FOR FIVE CENTURIES the wooden beams of the Bull and Firkin have been steeped in beer and village gossip. Heartbreak has soaked into the oak along with the jokes and harvest songs. The pub has seen scores of failed harvests and thousands of pints have been raised to departed friends under its low ceilings. Romantic tragedies that seemed world ending to the two, or three, or sometimes four people involved have been talked through in the fire lit rooms. Some ended with punches, some with kisses, but all had ended. Such were my thoughts as I took my first sip of beer and let its foaming magic recast my problems and Bella's as just the latest sentence in the ever lengthening chronicle of Wittleshin.

The evening passed slowly and uneventfully. Lupin made his way out of the kitchen and joined us after the last of the diners had been served their double chocolate puddings. We chatted about witches, home trees, disastrous dates and more. The teasing conversation of old friends is the best medicine for a troubled soul. Anxieties are blunted by familiar jokes and well worn stories from a shared past. Bella and her brother did not need to reassure me about Lorna's blackmail threat, just telling them about it recast it as a comic absurdity, something the three of us would get through together and would one day laugh about over wine and a dish that Lupin had not yet even dreamed of. I hope that in return our gentle ribbing told Bella that she would not die alone, that if she never made it Marrakesh she would always have us and Wittleshin and the Bull and Firkin.

The sun was still lingering low on the horizon when I left the pub to a chorus of goodbyes. The summer solstice and the longest day of the year were just a few days away and the evenings were long and quiet. I drifted towards Pentdown Hall and decided that this sense of beery bliss was too good to waste in my little cottage. I would take a stroll up to Beech Ridge and watch the light fade from the valley.

3

The turnoff to Beech Ridge was opposite Pentdown Hall's long tree-lined driveway. It was a narrow track, overgrown with grass except for two strips where the tyres of the occasional tractor or Land Rover wore away the vegetation. I walked briskly, enjoying the summer air and the warming effect of the ale in my belly. I was hoping to reach the top of the ridge in time to see the sun go down behind Wittleshin's picturesque church spire. It is a sight I have seen thousands of times, but like a favourite face it only gets better with familiarity.

Honeysuckle festooned the hedgerows and the air of the lane was thick with its lily-sweet smell. I stopped and plucked a flower, and, pulling off the long corolla, dabbed the bead of sugary dew onto my tongue, enjoying the treat as much as I had when I first learnt the trick as a young sapling. It was as reassuring as Lupin's grin and Bella's laugh, telling me that no matter how the world changed some things would always remain. The taste and fragrance of woodbine would linger in these parts long after my tree had fallen, be that to the developers' bull-dozers, a strike of lightning or the slow colonisation of beetles and fungus.

I opened the five-bar gate at the end of the lane and entered the woods. In the dying light the grey trunks of the beech trees rose like the pillars of a temple. The ground beneath was soft with last year's leaves. I expected to be alone; most walkers would be back in their houses by now, but to my surprise I heard distant sounds of music and laughing from deep amongst the trees.

As I reached the big clearing, which each spring was carpeted with bluebells, the source of the noise was clear. Around the edge of the circular space caravans were parked. These were not the beige and grey motorhomes of the retired pensioner. They were glossy in bright greens, yellows, reds and orange. Painted animals cavorted across their high sides. The caravan closest to me was decorated with a vast grinning pig in a bowler hat, its nose pointed skywards as it skipped along. Like wagons in the Old West they were circled around a roaring campfire. Silhouetted against the flames I could see the outlines of musicians; a fiddle player, a drummer, and a flautist. The tune they played was an ancient one. I recognised it from distant harvest days in centuries long forgotten. I hovered on the edge of the troop, forgetting about the sunset, losing myself in the music of years gone by.

My eyes were closed. I tapped my feet along to the half familiar rhythm and did not notice the child until she spoke.

"What are you doing here?" she demanded, with the

confidence of the very young. The girl was so blond that her hair was almost silver. Were it not for her dark eyebrows she could have been an albino.

"I'm just listening to the music," I said.

"But why?" Her voice was high and sounded like an instrument in itself.

"For same reason they are playing it, because it sounds nice." I smiled down at the child. There was something odd about her. She was too small and delicate, appearing not quite real.

"You shouldn't be listening to our music. Outsiders aren't supposed to hear the tunes. My Da says so."

I looked at the girl, with her large slanting eyes and pale skin, it was clear what she was. "I'm not an outsider, not really. I'm like you," I said.

"No you're not! Your skin is all dark and your hands are rough. You're lying! Da says you people always lie." She began to shout. "Da, Da, there's someone watching us, Da, come quick we are being watched by a liar."

Her shouts stopped the music and a group of seven or eight men came running from the clearing. They all shared the young girl's bright, white hair and dark, heavy eyebrows. Some of them held violins others large sticks made from a wood whose grain I did not recognise. One of them stood taller than the rest, towering above his companions as he advanced, though the top of his head could not have been higher than my armpits. He bent and told the child: "It's all right Esmy, go find your mother." As the child ran off he turned to look at me.

"Don't you know better than to spy on a gypsy camp, Gadjo? We're dangerous people. We can make things difficult for outsiders like you."

"I wasn't spying," I said. "I'm just out for a walk and stopped to hear you play, and you are not gypsies, so don't go pretending you are."

The small pale man looked indignant. "Of course we're gypsies! Look at the caravans. Look!" He threw out his arm. The clearing was darkening but the painted animals seemed to glow with their own light. On the side of the caravan beyond the man's outstretched finger a giant mouse in a tutu balanced on a red and green chequered ball. It twitched its nose and winked at me.

"You are not gypsies. Your caravan just winked at me." I said.

"We are living in the woods for goodness' sake. Gypsies is as gypsies does, and we are gypsies through and through."

The beer I had drunk earlier made me bolder than I might otherwise have been. "You are not gypsies. I've met your type before, but not for years. You are the Fae, fairy folk."

The tiny men erupted in a chorus of unconvincing snorts and faked laughs. "No such thing as fairies," shouted their leader, in a voice that seemed to tinkle like a wind chime. "We're gypsies to the marrow, vagabonds the lot of us. We'll steal your horses and your wheelbarrows! Now get away from here."

I decided it was best to meddle no further. The fairy folk must have a reason for being in Wittleshin, and a motive for keeping themselves secret, but it was not my business to pry. Strange things happened to those who became too involved in the lives of the Fae.

I put my hands up. "Okay, you are gypsies. I believe you. Now I must go, enjoy the rest of your night."

I turned and carried on walking up the hill. I could hear no one following, but fairies are light on their toes, and a single leaf wouldn't have rustled if the whole camp was on my heels. The old folk in our parts still told stories of the Fae and of the young boys and girls who they tempted away to join them. What happened to these human recruits was a mystery. None of the folk in the clearing looked like they had once been a Wittleshin farm labourer; we tended to specialise in broad faced and sunburned lads with honest grins, people who more resembled the smiling pig in the hat than those who had painted it. After a few hundred yards I turned to see the crowd of fairies standing where I'd left them, staring up the hill towards me, glowing in the dusk like luminescent mushrooms.

My detour and the music had stolen the best part of sunset, but I considered myself lucky. The old legends told of whole lifetimes lost to the haunting fairy pipes. Despite the encroaching gloom from the ridge I still had an impressive view of the village, its stones turned glorious gold by the last of the orange light.

Below the last rooks flying home to their messy nests Wittleshin looked tiny and perfect. The small cluster of buildings was dominated by the church spire, which faced off across the Village Green with the ramshackle roofline of the Bull and Firkin. In the centre of the Green the pond had drawn down all the lurid colour of the evening sky. Marbled streaks of grey, orange and purple that were broken and warped by the V-shaped ripples made by cruising ducks.

I switched my attention from the centre of Wittleshin, looking over the red tiled roof of the village hall and across the fields to Pentdown Hall. There, past the formal gardens and down beyond the meadow, my gnarled home tree stood black in front of the waving grass.

The view did not lend me its serenity. I felt on edge once more, as if I were being watched. I scanned the dark of the tree line and saw that I was not alone. A man was with me on the Ridge, half concealed by the shadows of the beeches. He leant on a fence. His elbows were bent, his hands at his temples. His eyes briefly flashed with the lurid orange of the sunset, the glass lenses of a pair of binoculars catching the sunset and flashing it back to me. I followed the line of his gaze and saw that he was focused on my home tree.

"Have you seen anything interesting?" I asked, hoping he was a simple birdwatcher and nothing more. "I hear there was a marsh warbler spotted down by the river last week."

The man said nothing, just kept staring down at my oak. I didn't recognise him as a villager. He was grey-haired and balding with a huge belly that bulged out over the waistband of his mustard-yellow corduroy trousers.

"Have you seen anything interesting?" I repeated, walking over and tapping the man on the shoulder. Although it was only the lightest of touches it sent his body pivoting around the fence post, wheeling as he fell sideways. He landed on his back, his arms rigid, still holding the binoculars to his eyes. His face was bright blue and he was very, very dead.

4

I sat in my living room, surrounded by botanical prints and cold climate orchids. A visitor once skewered my home decor as that of a Georgian antiquarian brought low by gin, a perceptive description and one that was more kind than cruel. I had picked a book at random from the shelves of tomes and curios that lined the walls but it sat open and ignored on my lap. The unread book and I were waiting for the unlovable Inspector Davies, who had promised to call and update me as soon as they had conducted the initial search around Beech Ridge. I felt I knew what the policeman would tell me; that the man had died of a suspected heart attack, and that they had found no suspicious circumstances so were handing matters to the coroner. There was no way a local police service such as ours, or any police service for that matter, would recognise the symptoms of elf violet poisoning.

The blue face was the major giveaway, along with the almost instant stiffening into rigor mortis. The man had frozen in the position in which he had died, binoculars aloft, staring down at my spirit tree. It was enough to make me shiver, as if someone had walked over my grave. The responsibility for the man's death could only lie with me. I had shared a deadly plant with a witch and she had not even waited an afternoon before she started killing.

An enthusiastic pounding on the door ended my wait. Inspector Davies would never be trusted lead an armed raid, something he made up for it in his house calls.

"Hello, hello! Anybody home?" cried Inspector Davies. There was a manic momentum to his voice, as if he had been shouting all night and would not stop on my account. It wasn't often that Wittleshin police station had a dead body come in. Our last recorded crime was an incident of petty vandalism. Someone had sprayed 'MOST WIVES ARE PSYCHOTIC' on the wall of the scout hut. We had debated suspects and motives in the Bull and Firkin for weeks. Skinny Joe Pike and Steve the Plumber had argued that the act was wrong but the sentiment probably wasn't. I had wondered if it was a coded message, some sort of anagram, after all, wouldn't 'MY WIFE IS PSYCHOTIC' be a more powerful piece of graffiti, or even 'MY WIVES ARE PSYCHOTIC' for the village bigamists. I had let the police know my theory, suggesting that 'MOSCOW PRIVY AESTHETICS' was the most likely solution, and that perhaps it might be a comment by a disillusioned boy scout on the state of his hut, but they had been uninterested and had suspected that I was winding them up. A few weeks later the criminal had returned to add an 'I' to the first word of his statement, scuppering my theory and forcing the outraged ladies of the

Women's Institute to hold a fundraising coffee morning for a tin of white wash.

"The door is open, Inspector, come in," I called.

Davies barrelled into the room. He wore mirrored aviator sunglasses, Texas Rangers style, despite it being the middle of the night in rural England.

"Hello Mr Oak," he bellowed, his face red.

"Please, call me Bertie," I said. We had known each other for over ten years, and I saw him most weekends in the bar of the Bull and Firkin. For some reason my interest in police business and my constant questioning of his methods seemed to irritate him.

"Not while I'm on duty," replied the policeman, snapping off his shades and giving me what I assume he thought to be an authoritative stare.

"I'll start with the good news Mr Oak, we are not arresting you. You are free to go."

Go where? I was already at home. "Well that's a relief," I said, pandering to Davies' inflated view of himself. "Are you going to arrest anyone?"

"At this moment we are not looking for any suspects and the death is not being treated as suspicious," he said, speaking straight from the police officers' training manual. "I am here to provide you with support and information following what..." he looked blank for a moment and mouthed some silent words, testing them out before he shared them "...following..., following... Following what must have been an upsetting and traumatic discovery!" He smiled, pleased at having delivered his speech so commandingly, then cleared his throat. "Mr Oak. Are. You. Alright?"

"I'm fine. It gave me a bit of a shock, though. I thought he was alive, I'd been talking to him."

"Yes, funny that wasn't it, the way he just died leaning up there. We think it was a heart attack, but we don't know for sure. They're going to do a post-mortem and send samples off for toxicity testing. Just like on the television. Although you can't tell anyone I told you that. It is an official police secret. If I find myself reading about anything I have just said then I shall have no choice but to arrest you."

I doubted whether even in an area as starved for news as ours the papers would be interested in the headline *'Police Suspect Fat Man Died of Heart Attack.'* And it wasn't the kind of material I covered in my column, though wild tangents are the Garden Writers best friend and I've written about worse.

"Don't worry Inspector, I wouldn't dare say a word. Do we have any idea who he might have been? I didn't recognise him. Not someone from the village?"

"No," said Davies. "A stranger. We couldn't find any ID on him, but he had a receipt in his pocket from the Bull and Firkin. I'm going down there tomorrow to see if anyone remembers him. I might go undercover."

An undercover trip to the village pub where everyone knew him, there were worse ways to earn some overtime pay.

"Then I'll go and see those gypsies who've set up camp on the ridge. I've been waiting for a chance to get my hands on them. God, I hate gypsies. If I had my way..." He trailed off into bronchial muttering.

"Yes, you've told me your views on gypsies before. You give them what for, eh?" I said, standing up and clapping him on the shoulder. It gave me some pleasure to think of the trouble The Fae would give him. "But if it's not a murder what are you going to accuse them of?"

Davies laughed unpleasantly. His toad-like presence in my second favourite arm chair did not agree with the botanical gentleman ambience of my living room. Even in the flattering light of my rackety brass table lamp his face was florid and sweaty. I wished he would leave.

I briefly considered telling Inspector Davies my suspicion that he was dealing with a poisoning, but thought better of it. I had checked the plants earlier and by the light of my torch there didn't seem to be any obvious bits of the elf violet missing, neither from the one on my plot nor in the one I had taken up to Lorna in the big house, though that didn't mean a few leaves hadn't been whisked away, or a tiny fraction of the roots snipped off. The most minuscule quantity in the wrong hands was all that was needed to kill a man, but the forensics teams would not have the equipment to test for it and reporting a witch and a death by mythical plant would only make me look like a lunatic. Besides, getting into all that would require the Inspector to stay longer.

No, it was better to keep the police out. If it was elf violet then the suspects in this murder would be Lorna, the fairies, who knew all about the power of elf violet, and me. We were all supernatural things and mixing us with an official investigation could only lead to trouble. I might not have solved the case of the scout hut sprayer, but this looked like it was shaping up to be another case for Albertus Oak. I would go up to the big house and ask Lorna Brimtide some serious questions, just as soon as I could get rid of the policeman.

"Was there anything else Inspector Davies?" I yawned. "I'm afraid it was rather traumatic finding the body like that. I'm feeling slightly frazzled and I think it's probably best if I go bed."

"Well..." There was one more thing, said Davies, looking suddenly shy. "...It's about my clematis?"

IF ONLY ALL life's mysteries were as easy to solve as that of Davies' non flowering clematis; after interrogation it emerged that he was pruning a group three plant as if it were group one, cutting the buds off before they had a chance to form.

It had taken me some time to explain the cause to the policeman, who would not accept it as a problem of his own making and left my house saying that he was going to buy some more bug spray, he had, after all, seen a caterpillar in his garden. By the time I set out to Pentdown Hall it was already gone midnight, long past the accepted hour for social calls on one's boss. In all the years I had worked for Sir Lionel Brimtide I had never disturbed him after nine. Though in the decades I had spent gardening for that old man I rarely had reason to suspect him of poisoning anyone. Still, I wasn't concerned about waking Lorna, most witches I'd known over the years had been night owls. The greater danger lay in disturbing her. Any animal that find's itself stepped on is liable to bite. As a precaution I stopped at the old twisted hazel that stood at the gate of my cottage and searched amongst its branches for one of the rare double cob-nuts that were said to ward off members of the dark covens.

My nerve almost failed at the doorway of the stately home. A purple fog drifted out past the hinges. Each wisp lingered in the glow of the iron lantern before creeping up into the night. Pentdown's main door was adorned with a snarling brass leopard's head, the heraldic beast of the Brimtide's. In its mouth it clasped a heavy knocker which I raised and let fall against the door. After a few moments the door opened. In a cloud of sweet-smelling mist stood Lorna Brimtide. She wore a dark shimmering garment in silk or satin and seemed dressed for a place far more glamorous that Wittleshin at midnight. One of her dark eyebrows was raised, but there was nothing in her expression that said she was annoyed to have been disturbed, indeed, nothing to say she was even surprised.

We stood in silence while the unnatural smoke rolled around her.

"Mr Oak!" She exclaimed, eventually. Settling on a bright enthusiastic tone that was inappropriate for both time and circumstance. The voice of an overworked teacher whose coffee break has been disturbed by a curious child. "I do so love a man who is enthusiastic about his role. You must be as excited as me about our plans for the new gardens. I haven't been able to think about anything else either. Have you had any more thoughts on the long border?"

"No."

"Oh." She seemed momentarily confused. "So this is a social call? Well... do come in." She waved her hands trying to create a passage through the swirling mists.

"Don't worry about the smoke. I'm experimenting for my new line," she said.

"A new line in what?"

"Aromatherapy. This one is going to be called *Lilacs from Dead Ground.*"

"Aromatherapy?"

"Yes, using scents to soothe and heal. You'd be surprised how many problems can be fixed by the right smell."

"You are not an aromatherapist." I said.

"I'm an aromatherapist as much as you're a gardener. Although I suppose you might call me a *perfumier.*"

"I know what you are."

Lorna gave me a long steady look. I returned her gaze and we stood on the door step while a moth dashed between us to batter at the light. "So what am I?" said Lorna, eventually.

"You are a witch."

Lorna's large dark eyes broke from mine, then rose again in a challenging stare.

"Don't worry," I said. "I'm not the ducking type, I have no problem in principle with your sort. Just tell me; what are really doing? What is this?" I waved at the vapour floating from behind her. Now that I was aware of it it did smell of lilacs, but there was another sweetness, a mouldering smell, complex, mushroomy and not all together pleasant.

"I really am making a new scent. This is how I earn my money. This scent is supposed to heat this place and fix the roof. I'm afraid, Mr Oak, that dancing naked round a cauldron doesn't pay the bills." She paused. "Well it does actually, but that's not the kind of money I want to make. Yes I'm a witch, very astute of you to work it out. But a witch has to diversify now days, we need to be business women. There really wasn't much call for all the old eye-of-newt stuff up in London so now I flog smelly candles."

"Doesn't that get boring? Don't you ever feel the call?"

"What call?"

"The call of your dark master!"

Loran laughed. "I think you've misread me. I was never a satanic pact kind of girl, worse luck, as it does look fun. I would never be able to manage the child killing."

"What about adult killing?"

"Oh yes, lots of that, sign me up!"

"Really?"

"No! My God, no. Look, why are here? What's the point of all this?"

I decided that it would be best to get straight to the point. "I found a body."

"You found what?"

"I found a body, a dead body. A man."

I studied her closely. She seemed genuinely appalled. There was real shock and horror in her eyes.

"Where?" she asked. "Not in the gardens?"

"No. Not in the gardens, out on the ridge. A middle-aged guy, fat. Not from round here."

"How horrible for you, Albertus. I really am sorry. Have you told the police?"

Sensible questions. "Yes, they think that he probably died of a heart attack."

Lorna gave me a kind look, one designed to suggest that she knew how the death must have shaken me, and that if I was in need of company and a sympathetic ear I could count on her. "I know how hard these things can be," she said. "Why don't you come inside and tell me all about it? I can make you a hot chocolate, or I have sloe gin if you prefer something stronger, or some arnica maybe?"

There was no way I was accepting anything edible, not with an elf-violet-poisoner on the loose. "I don't need a hot chocolate, Lorna, and I'm fine. There was something else I wanted to tell you about, well warn you about really. The police think he had a heart attack, but I don't. I think he was murdered."

"Murdered? What makes you think that?"

"His face was blue." I paused. Lorna was stony faced. "Elf violet blue," I prompted.

She coughed. "Oh," she said after a moment. "And... you think this has something to do with me? Albertus, no. I wanted the elf violet but I would never do anything like that with it. I'm not that type of witch. I couldn't do harm to anything or anyone. I wouldn't. It's not in my nature. I'm the sleep potions and good luck charms type. I cast spells to find lost earrings or to heal the blisters from your tight shoes. I don't poison people."

Her words did not ring true. She seemed too well put together and sleek to be a thaumaturgic chiropodist. Bella Lestrade, who spent time on insalubrious internet forums, had told me that there were layers of the supernatural that us rural beings had never heard of. A few months earlier she had excitedly whispered about a secret chamber under the garden of Number 10 Downing Street where young city witches were taken to write charmed PR and magically influence the value of Sterling. Apparently every Prime Minister was allowed to transform two people into newts, no questions asked, which explained the Leader of the Opposition. The stories were most likely nonsense but in situations such as this, where bodies spoiled my beautiful hills, it was wise to to take heed of the conspiracy theorists and question everything.

"And anyway," continued Lorna. "If I were to kill anyone I wouldn't do it three hours after acquiring the poison. I'd wait a week or two," She smiled and placed a conciliatory arm on mine. Her touch gave me goosebumps.

"I'd better let you know. I'll be keeping my eyes open. I'm going to do my very best to find out what has been going on," I said, gruffly, before turning away and starting back towards my cottage.

"Albertus," called Lorna. I faced her again. "Thank you. It makes me feel better to know that someone as good as you is out here looking into things. I appreciate it."

She smiled and closed the door, leaving me alone with the almost full moon and the summer moths.

5

The next day I woke early, unable to sleep longer despite my late night. From my bed I made straight for the garden. Daybreak on a summer's morning is an almost religious experience for me. There is a sense of calm anticipation in the still-cold air, a promise of wondrous things ahead. But that day felt different. I was anxious, too on edge to enjoy the sight of the cobwebs shimmering in the dewy grass or the pink tinged sky to the east. In such an agitated state there was no way I could work on the intellectually draining tasks of redesigning the long border and working out what to do about the roses, so I busied myself in vigorous, unthinking physical labour. I would see to the compost heaps and the mulching.

First, I went to the comfrey beds and harvested great handfuls of the rough green leaves. Sir Lionel Brimtide had once used a German carpenter who showed me how to fry them in golden batter to make Bavarian *Schwarzwurz*, and when I was a young apprentice gardener I had been schooled in the herb's legendary bone-knitting properties. We seemed to have more broken bones in those days, when we rode around on horses and hay-carts and there was no such thing as a flashlight. Nowadays I grow it for the crude purpose of rotting down to fertilise the rest of the garden. It is a sacrificial crop, giving its life to the soil as I have given mine. Like the comfrey I have no need to write an autobiography, it's all there in the yew pyramids and espaliered apples, the story of my years.

I threw the leaves into an empty barrel and weighed them down with bricks. Gravity and decay would rot them into a thick black vegetable soup, stinking and nutritious, the perfect thing for roses, though I was sure that dog mercury and monksbane of the new regime would also appreciate it. The light work finished, I stopped for a restorative cup of tea before picking out my favourite ash handled fork and launching myself into the largest compost heap. I dug with mindless vigour through the stratified layers of vegetation, uncovering cities of worms and centipedes, relishing the earthy smell and the heat generated by the rotting matter. Often in the winter I would come to the heaps first thing in the morning as the sun rose to watch the hot mounds sending out plumes of steam into the cold air and smell their complicated aromas. The irony of using compost, the essence of death and decay, to distract me from the murder did not escape me, and I tried hard to stop myself imagining whether the body I had found would soon undergo a similar process.

The dead man and the fate of his remains were not the only intrusive thoughts at home in my head. I was tormented by visions of Lorna Brimtide and the smile she had given me the night before. Her face appeared to me again and again to the soundtrack of yesterday's haunting fairy fiddle. I tried to divert energy away from my brain and into my muscles and by mid-morning I ached with the strain of heaving compost and soil.

The sun grew hotter and I stripped to the waist, before taking my lunch in the shade of a large sycamore. Birds sang in the branches above me and bees buzzed lazily up and away again. It felt strange to sit in such pleasant tranquillity whilst knowing that in a few hours I would again be investigating a murder. I had decided to revisit Beech Ridge.

MY BODY WAS STARTING to ache from the morning's work as I reached the Bull and Firkin. I leant back and stretched my arms wide, feeling the tightness across my chest and enjoying it. I rolled my neck, stood up on tiptoes and groaned. Stretches completed I walked into the pub. Before I could reach the bar Bella started shouting excitedly.

"Bertie! Exciting news! You know that man I went on a date with yesterday?"

"The racist?"

"That's the one! Well he's dead! Inspector Davies came in to see us. They found him up on Beech Ridge, and he still had the receipt from our lunch in his pocket."

She seemed improperly excited. I thought goths were supposed to be into the solemn sanctity of death. She looked as happy as a morris dancer.

"So no second date then?" I asked.

"Not likely. Inspector Davies said he had a heart attack, but I've been telling Lupin it was his food that killed him."

"Is Lupin here?" I asked.

She nodded, "He's at the stove, trying to burn us all to the ground again."

"Flaming cherry cake?"

"Afraid so," said Bella

"Get him out of the kitchen. I need to talk to him."

"What's got into you Albertus? You've come over all forceful." She laughed and headed off in search of the chef.

I drummed my fingers on the bar and waited. Bella emerged dragging her frowning brother by the coat sleeves. "What is it Bertie? I've got fifteen beef Wellington to wrap," he said. Lupin's chef's whites were spattered with pink and he smelled strongly of kirsch.

"What did you cook for the man who died?" I asked, in a more aggressive voice than I had intended to use.

Lupin looked slightly shocked. "Aw, Bertie. I can't remember; it was a busy lunchtime. I don't see who eats what, I just cook it. Why?"

"I don't think he had a heart attack. I think he was poisoned."

"Very funny Bertie. Bella's already made all those jokes."

"I'm serious Lupin. I was the one who found him. I'm almost certain that his death was not of natural causes. Tell me what he ate."

Bella answered for him. "I remember what he ate. He

had steak cooked rare with triple fried oven chips, no salad, and he ate it all with his mouth open."

I turned to Lupin. "The steak, does it have a marinade?"

"No, it doesn't need one. Well-aged Aberdeen Angus isn't a flavour I'm going to muck about with." He huffed.

"No sauce, no herb crust, nothing went out to him but meat and potatoes?"

"That's right Poirot," said Lupin grumpily. He did not like any criticism of his food, well-founded or otherwise.

I told them about finding the body, about the man's blue face, his hands clamped around the binoculars, and about elf violet, a plant that they knew from nursery rhymes. Both were shocked to hear it actually existed and grew in the village of Wittleshin.

"What do you know about the man, Bella? What did he tell you? Did he seem worried about anything? Did he mention any enemies? A gambling debt maybe?"

"Well, I sort of tuned out after the whole racist incident. Hey, maybe the Moroccans finally got him!" Bella laughed. "No, seriously, he mainly talked about his job."

"You mentioned his boring job, what was it?"

"He was a property developer. He said he was here because he had a meeting with some landowner, someone who was new to the area and was thinking of selling off some of their fields."

I felt cold. He could only have meant Lorna. So she had not been bluffing. My meadow could be sold. I remembered where the man had been staring when he died. He had been pointing his binoculars right at my spirit tree. Was it to be the site of Wittleshin's newest housing estate?

"Are you all right Bertie, you've gone awfully pale," said Lupin.

"I'm fine. I've just realised that I'm the main suspect."

"What on earth are you talking about?" asked the chef.

"That man wanted to buy Lorna's meadow, the one with my tree in it. I'm the person with the biggest motive for killing him."

They looked at me sceptically.

"And I'm the only person in the village who grows elf violet. I have the means of killing him as well!"

"Well... did you kill him?" asked Bella.

"No! Of course I didn't kill him."

"Then don't get so worked up about it, honestly you're worse than my brother. The police think it was a heart attack so they don't care, and the man was an arse, so we don't care. Lupin, make your cake, Bertie have a pint, bish bash bosh, another perfect day in Wittleshin."

"Someone died Bella." I said. "They were murdered which means there must be a murderer out there."

"Or in here," said Lupin, pointing at his sister.

"Or in here. Bella do you think you could come with me back up to the ridge?" I asked. "Have a snoop round with your extra-sensory perception? See if we can find any trails in the spirit world."

"Sure," Bella said. "Tomorrow morning? I'll have some time before we open up."

"No. It has to be tonight. We'll go after you have closed."

"I'm coming too," blustered Lupin. "If people really are getting murdered then you're going to need protection."

FROM THE ROAD the woods were dark and lifeless, an imposing black block against the starry sky. But as we crept closer stripes of orange flashed between the ancient tree trunks, becoming larger and brighter as we approached the caravans of the Fae. Far from being empty the clearing was filled with fire, song and high-pitched laughter. Magic or woodcraft had kept the fairy folk hidden from the few people who might tread the lanes of Wittleshin long after the pubs had closed but we were now too near for them to hide. Bella made a whispered argument for joining the silver-haired people in their revelry. She and Lupin were too young to remember the Fae's last party in our little village, and the boys and girls that had danced off with them. I told her: "Over my wood-wormed body."

Lupin said nothing. We paused in the root hollow of a blown down tree and for moments he did not even breathe. An owl hooted overhead and he exhaled in a short strangled scream.

"Lupin, you're supposed to be a werewolf. You're a creature of the bloody night. Why are you so scared?" hissed Bella to her brother, punching his arm.

"One night a month! The rest of the time I'm a chef. Chefs are not creatures of the night!" He sounded panicked. "Anyway what makes you think I'm scared?" whispered Lupin angrily. The owl called again and he grasped my arm hard.

"Let's get on." I said, choosing not to tell the Lestrades about the fairy folk and their haunting ability to inhabit the voices of other creatures. If they knew we were here it was better that we did not loiter around their camp.

We crested the brow of the hill. "This is where I found him." I gestured towards the fence post where the fat man had died. "You two search the area, don't make too much of a mess. I'll talk to the trees."

Some gardeners are so attuned to the natural world that plants almost seem to speak to them. They can hear the water gurgling in the xylem tubes of a shrub, they can put their ear against a trunk and know whether it is rotting, just from the tone and timbre of the creaks. I was not one of those gardeners. Plants didn't just seem to speak to me, they genuinely did speak to me.

This was not such a boon as it might seem in investigating murders. Plants are generally very unobservant. They don't have eyes so they only really notice things that touch them. The woody plants that might live for hundreds of years spend most of their time in a semi-permanent coma, a persistent vegetative state, and for annuals who live and die in a single year time passes so quickly that they are hard pressed to remember anything that happened more than five minutes previously.

I made my way to the nearest of the beech trees that gave the ridge its name. Not all vegetation was created equal, and not all plants were equally chatty. I remembered, from past conversations, that beech trees were notoriously slow and forgetful, but also that they could be vain and paranoid. They believed everyone was out to get the valuable truffles that sometimes grew amongst their roots.

I approached the trunk and placed both my palms on it, before leaning my forehead down to the smooth bark. I tried to force away the human parts of my consciousness and channel the tree within me.

"Hello," I projected.

I heard a bubbling deep in the tree's soft core as it woke from its slumber. Some trees went years without waking at all. We'd be lucky if this one sensed anything the night before.

The voice seemed to speak directly into my head, ancient and creaky, its vowels splintering. "Hello," it rumbled. "What do you want? Who are you?"

"Albertus Oak. I'm a dryad. I'd like to ask you some questions."

There was a long pause and eventually the tree spoke again.Its voice was slow.

"I don't like dryads," it said. "They are too wiggly."

"What do you mean too wiggly?" I mind channelled.

After this there was a long pause. I worried that the tree had slipped back into slumber, or had grown distracted by the squirming of a worm on its tiniest roots. Both of us would have been of equal importance and interest to the beech. Eventually the tree spoke again. "Too wiggly by half, claim to be trees but wiggle about like squirrels. Untrustworthy things. They eat truffles."

"I'm sorry you feel like that," I channelled. "You don't have to trust me, but would you mind answering a few questions? I'll not wiggle, and I promise I'm not hunting truffles."

"If I answer your questions will you leave me alone?"

"Yes."

"Then I suppose I will talk to you," the tree rumbled. "I'm sure you've asked all the other trees already, everyone does. They think of the oak and the ash and the holly, and even the horrible willow, and only when there is no one left they come and talk to us beech trees."

This was the classic beech tree persecution complex. I knew what was coming next: The Julius Caesar Monologue. We both waited in a silence that could have lasted decades. "I prefer beech trees to willows." I finally said.

"You know when Caesar came to Britain he said there were no beech trees here?" groaned the tree "None! He wrote it down in a book, made of paper. It's a lie. We were here. No one ever notices us, but we were here."

"I know you were here," I soothed. "You've been here just as long as the oak trees, and just as long as the horrible willow. I know all that. I want to ask you a question about last night."

"About last night? Is it summer?"

The tree paused. I could hear popping and clicking from its phloem tubes as it sent its consciousness out through limbs and bows to the very tips of its twigs. After a long time I felt its spirit return to the trunk.

"I've got my leaves on so it must be summer. I don't think I remember anything since last winter."

"Look right into the bottom of your roots and see if there's anything you can remember. I'm sure you are telling the truth, but just try it for me," I urged.

The beech creaked under the strain of remembering, probably the hardest work the great wooden plant had done since forcing its way from its seed case.

"Yes," murmured the tree. "I remember something. Last night something climbed in me. Something sat in my branches. Not owl, not wiggly squirrel, something bigger, something human-shaped. They were there for a half a quarter spin."

Trees had no understanding of hours, they measured time in days and seasons. A spin was a day, a quarter spin was six hours, half a quarter spin was three hours. "Can you remember anything else?"

"No, just human shape. Half a quarter spin."

"Thank you," I projected. "I've always said that the beech was the most useful of all the trees. Much better than the willow."

"You tell that to Caesar," murmured the tree and I felt it drifting back into a deep-rooted sleep.

So someone had been here. I wondered if they had been looking at me as I found the body. The thought gave me a chill.

"Bertie! I think we have found something." Bella's excited voice came from the darkness. I rushed over to where she and her brother knelt by the fence post. Lupin's electric torch illuminated the base of the post and on it a carved band of ornate symbols, tiny triangles dots and squiggles.

"What language is it?" I asked.

Bella, who like most pub landlords considered herself something of a scholar, stroked her chin. "I've never seen anything like it, could be runic, or elfish, perhaps some ancient form of Wiccan. I really don't know."

I thought of the people down the hill. "Could it be the language of the Fae?"

6

"Go and check the other fence posts," I told Lupin.

He gave me an imploring look, not wanting to head out into the dark. Bella questioned his manliness and he did as I suggested. After tramping for twenty yards he shouted back. "There's nothing on this one." His footfalls grew fainter and his voice farther off. "Nor this one. I think yours is the only one with carvings. It's the murder post for sure. Can I come back now?"

"I can feel something," Bella whispered. "There's a presence here I'm sure of it. I am picking up some strong energy from the spirit world."

"What is it? A ghost maybe?"

"I don't know. The energy feels strange, confused almost. It's buzzing around on the edge of my brain like a forgotten chore. I think it wants to make itself known but it can't. Either it's too weak or I'm not a strong enough medium."

"Where is it? Is it coming from over by the fence post?" I pressed.

"It's all around us." Bella's voice was strange, like she was speaking from a long way away. She was focussing hard on the spirit world, half her consciousness was in a realm those of us without the Sight could barely even comprehend. "I can't get it to focus in one place. It won't stay still. It's restless."

There was frustration in Bella's voice. "No, it's no use, we can't connect. I think I need something to amplify it with. Lupin!" she shouted. "Get back here Lupin."

We heard his heavy steps as he joined us from the gloom.

"I need you to go back to the inn, head up to my room. In the top drawer of my dresser there is a crystal ball. Bring it back here."

Her brother thus instructed she turned to me. "Bertie, I need you to find me some strong twigs of rowan, at least five of them."

I turned to walk into the woods, having long ago learnt that when Bella made her mind up about something it was best to go along with it.

This was behaviour Lupin should have learned in childhood, still he tried to fight it. "That's not fair," he protested. "Why should I go all the way back on my own? It's so dark out there. I'll find the twigs instead."

"Can you recognise a rowan tree?" Bella asked.

"No."

"Then go and get the crystal ball."

I could tell it pained Lupin to be so craven, but the dark of the night and the words carved in the unrecognisable language had spooked him. "Maybe you could come with me Bella?" he suggested. "I might not find the crystal ball on my own, your room is such a mess."

"Nice try, but I need to prepare a safe area up here, it's going to be hard. I've never done anything like this before. Just go you scaredy-wolf."

Lupin clumped back down the hill muttering and swinging his torch beam.

I turned to Arabella. "Are you sure you can manage this?" Her bond with the spirit world was fragile at best. Unpredictable events happened when she groped behind the veil of consciousness, and this was well beyond experimenting with tea leaves back at the Bull and Firkin.

"I don't really know," said Bella. "But what's the worst that could happen?"

THE NIGHT WAS warm and thick with noise. These were the months of sun, when night was at its shortest and all the deeds of the after-dark were squeezed into a half dozen hours. Something small scurried to our left and was jumped on by a heavier animal. There was a squeal and a yip. It was a reminder that our murder was just one item in Beech Ridge's summer of death. To the dryads that had walked the Whit Valley when my wood still was green a human life was like a vole's — utterly lacking in dignity and consequence. But those old tree gods were gone. I was alone and had grown sappy and soft towards mankind. I even loved some of them.

Bella arranged the five rowan branches I had cut from the woods into a rough pentangle and used another twig to scrape a crude circle into the surrounding dirt. She explained that if we sat inside the magical designs they would protect us, or was it if we sat in between them? She couldn't quite remember but assured me that if whatever spirit she called up turned out to be malicious then having a circle and a pentangle about could only be a good thing.

I shook my head. It was not what I had envisaged when I suggested heading up to Beech Ridge to investigate. I had been thinking of footprints in the mud and maybe a fragment of distinctive cloth caught on the barbed wire, perhaps a monogrammed handkerchief or an unstamped train ticket to Penzance. Something that said, unequivocally, clue.

Bella and I sat in silence, both preoccupied with our thoughts. Lupin returned, out of breath and carrying the crystal ball. The unbearded portions of his face were white and bloodless.

"See that wasn't so bad," said Bella.

Lupin cursed.

"Okay, both of you, come and sit with me," commanded the psychic, patting the ground inside the dirt circle and wooden pentagram. She took the heavy sphere and put it between us. "Now let's all hold hands."

We did she told us, forming a little triangle of arms around the glassy orb.

"So? Do we chant then? Isn't that what we normally do? Enact a Wiccan ritual, or perhaps do a dance?" said Lupin, braver now he was back with us.

"No," said Bella. "Just sit still and try not to get frightened. I will do all the work."

We existed silently for a while. An owl hooted and some dried deadwood fell from a nearby tree. Lupin rolled his eyes. He had little patience for his sister's predictions and prophecies. He would soon declare that he had had enough of this. I noticed the corners of his lips twitching into a telltale scowl which was strange, because I shouldn't have been able to see the corners of his lips on a moonless night. Between our arms the crystal ball was glowing with an otherworldly green light.

"What is that?" asked Lupin, the fear back in his voice. "What on Earth is that?"

It was Bella's turn to sound scared. "I don't know," she said. "It's never done that before. Perhaps the spirit that wanted to talk is in the ball."

"I doubt that," I said, looking up. Above our heads a vortex of green light was forming. It was like some distant nebula viewed through a telescope. A mass of twinkling points and spiralling, viridian arms. There was a small hole, like the eye of a hurricane, directly above the crystal ball, around which more and more light gathered, until the whole of Beech Ridge was illuminated in an eerie green.

Bella's tone was panicked. "Stay inside the circle! don't stop holding hands. I don't think I can control it." A wind whipped through the clearing, tugging at the boughs and clashing them together. I craned my neck, looking for any branches that might fall on us. To my horror I saw a pale face peering at us from between the trees.

"There's something there!" I shouted, the wind whipping away my words. We all turned to look. There was a creature out in the woods, its pale face low to the ground, its eyes shadowed into huge dark pits by the ectoplasmic light.

"Is it a ghost?" roared Lupin over the gale. "I've never seen a ghost look so real."

"It's not a ghost," I called, realising who the face belonged to. "It's one of the Fae. Go! Get back to your camp, it's not safe here!" The fairy did not have the protection of the rowan wood or the dirt circle. To a malevolent sprit it would have stood out like a church spire in a lightning storm.

Above our heads the maelstrom of green energy gathered itself into a swirling ball of light before arcing like a thunderbolt out and down. It struck the fairy between the eyes with a force that knocked the little creature backwards into the woods. The wind faded and left us in a darkness that felt a hundred times blacker than before.

We broke hands and ran to the tree line. I recognised the tiny fairy girl I had met the night before, Esmy. She lay on her back with her eyes closed and her arms splayed. Her fine silver hair spread out in disarray over last year's curling leaves. She appeared to have been struck dead.

Bella ran to her side and felt for a pulse. The fairy's neck was small and fragile under her human-sized hands. "Her heart is beating," said Bella. She put her cheek to the girl's tiny mouth. "And she's breathing. She might be in a spirit trance." She turned to her brother. "Lupin, I've got some Moroccan mint oil back at the Bull, run and get it." This time the werewolf did not complain and turned to hurry back down the hill, before we were all startled by a noise from Esmy the fairy-girl.

"I don't want no flaming Moroccan mint oil," she said in a deep voice. "I bloody hate Moroccans."

7

B ella threw another log on the fire, sending clouds of sparks up the Bull and Firkin's ancient brick chimney. Although it was mid summer the events on the ridge had left us with a chill that the apple-wood logs struggled to dispel. Lupin had set a pot of spiced cider on the hearth, and the sweet, warm liquid was putting colour in our faces and vigour in our conversation.

"Nope, no, no, no, nope. This ain't right," said Esmy, in a gruff Yorkshire accent. "Is this some sort of trick? Why won't any of you tell me what's going on."

"We can't tell you what's going on because we don't really know ourselves." I explained. "Listen to me Esmy..."

"That's not my name," interrupted the fairy.

"Sorry. We think we might have accidentally called you down into this body," I continued. Despite the gravity of the situation I was struggling not to laugh every time the tiny silver-haired child opened her mouth and spoke with the voice of a disgruntled man.

"Why am I so short?" demanded the fairy child. "Something is not right. You fellows are mucking me about. This is not my body!"

"I wouldn't complain. I'd say it's a fair improvement on your old body," said Bella, a trifle cruelly given the circumstances.

"I don't know what you're talking about young lady. A fine figure of a man I am. A prime piece of Yorkshire beef."

"Prime beef? You looked more like porkpie to me," she replied.

The fairy squinted at the scowling barmaid, scratching its chin. "I remember you. You're from the internet. We lunched together."

"We did."

"I know what has happened then, it all makes sense now," said the fairy.

"You do?" I asked, relieved that at least one person might have an idea what on earth was going on.

"I most certainly do. She's drugged me, that's what happened." A tiny accusatory finger was pointed at Bella. "She slipped something in my chips so she could have her wicked way with me. I've read about people like her. I knew I should never have gone for lunch with someone called Bella, it's not even a real name."

Bella laughed at the absurdity of the suggestion. "I didn't spike you. That would be a waste of drugs. And as far as any name can be real, Bella is."

The little man-in-a-fairy's-body remained calm. It sat on a cushion with its arms folded and its bottom lip stuck out, pleased to have sussed out what was going on. "I'll let you know something for nothing, love, better women than you have tried to trap me, and better women than you have failed. In a few hours I'll wake up sober and you'll still be a lonely internet weirdo."

Bella twitched. A vague and malevolent energy was throbbing from her direction. This, I thought, was how poltergeists were created. I stepped in before things got messy. "Mr...?" I asked. "Mr...? I'm sorry I don't know your name"

"Hipperty, Geoffrey Hipperty of the Harrogate Hippertys. You'll have heard of us no doubt."

"Yes, a most distinguished family," I said. I'd never encountered the name before, but the poor man deserved a little flattery. "Mr Hipperty, I'm afraid there was some kind of accident." I said, having decided to tell it to him straight.

"What do you mean lad? Come on, out with it." Mr Hipperty tossed a lock of hair away from his tiny porcelain-white forehead.

"Well, Mr Hipperty, there is no easy way to put this. You died."

"I did not," he said, stubbornly.

"You did. I found your body."

"Well boy, how come I'm talking to you now?"

"Well how come you have the body of a young female fairy? There are lots of things we need to understand, but one thing I'm clear on is that you are dead. Your body has been passed to the local coroner. Now, tell me, what do you remember about yesterday?"

"I'm not dead. I think I would remember dying. I'm on a drug induced freak-out."

"Okay, let's agree to differ for the time being. If we are going to find out whether she did drug you then you have to tell us what you remember about yesterday afternoon."

"Yesterday?" The tiny fairy scratched her chin again, a hangover from more stubbly days. "Hmm yesterday... Before she spiked me or after?" He nodded at Bella, who rolled her eyes in response.

"Both," I said.

"It were a fine morning. I stopped at Newport Pagnell Services for a fry up; bacon, eggs, beans, black pudding, the whole works. Lovely it was, I had a hash brown too. Of course it wasn't as good as a proper Yorkshire fry up, but then, what is?"

"Are you sure it wasn't a heart attack Bertie?" muttered Lupin. I hushed him.

"Please, Mr Hipperty, continue. What else do you remember?"

"Well, then I drove down to some middle-of-nowhere village, well they call it a village, no dry stone walls though. No idea what it was called, I'm afraid."

"Wittleshin?" I suggested.

"That's right. Wittleshin. I drove down to Wittleshin because I had a meeting with a woman; Laura? Lana? Lydia? I can't remember her name either, must be the drugs."

"Lorna?" I prompted.

"That's the blighter! Anyway, I knew I was coming down, so I found a nice picture of a boy who I thought had a bit of the Hipperty about him, not having any photos of myself to hand, and got on one of those Internet dating things, an app, to see if I couldn't find myself a bit of totty. What the wife don't know won't hurt

her, eh? Eh?" The little fairy girl leered and winked at
Bella. She looked away in disgust. "Eh?" said the fairy
again, trying to nudge Lupin in the ribs, but falling short
due to the exceptional shortness of her arms. "Ahh you're
no fun. Anyway, I had my lunch. Steak and chips, and
very nice it was too."

"Thanks," said Lupin.

"I could see that the date wern't going anywhere." He
turned his attention to Bella. "No offence love, but you
weren't really on my level. Most of the things I was
talking about were going straight over your head, and I
don't like black fingernails, they remind me of beetles."

Bella wriggled her black painted fingernails and
sneered.

Mr Hipperty scowled and turned the small child-like
face he now inhabited back to me: "So I decided I'd cut
my losses and scarper. Of course that was before I knew
that I had been drugged."

Bella started to say something but I cut her off with a
raised hand, keen to hear the end of the story before the
two of them came to blows.

"And where did you go after you left the pub?" I
asked.

"Well, I fancied something sweet. So I went next door
into the bakery."

"You know we serve puddings here," said Lupin.

"I know you do big man, and I'm sure they are lovely,
but like I said, I thought I should scarper."

"And what did you buy in the bakery, Mr Hipperty?" I
asked.

"Well I very nearly didn't buy anything at all. A right
old miserable sod that baker is. I was only trying to tell

him how in Yorkshire we make proper cream buns, not like these soft Southern ones you sell down here. I was informing him of Betty's Tea House, and the correct way to pipe custard and he started getting all huffy with me. He told me that if I didn't like his cream buns I could take a hike."

Bella and Lupin nodded in recognition. Mr Fairchild the baker was the most grumpy and argumentative man in the village. Years of getting up at three in the morning to load the oven, of being stung by wasps on the hunt for jam doughnuts, and of burning his fingers on red-hot baking trays, had singed all the goodness out of him and left him an angry husk of a man. But he did make exceptionally good cream buns.

"You missed out," said Lupin. "They may not be northern but they are best I've ever tasted. Though it's well-known round here that Mr Fairchild keeps the nicest for himself. You still should have bought one."

"Oh don't worry lad, I bought a bun in the end. The other customers in the queue told me that I should just ignore the baker and get one anyway. So I did."

"And how was it?" asked Lupin, his mind, as ever, on food.

"It were bloody delicious. I ate it as I walked up the hill. I still had a bit of time before my meeting with..."

"Lorna," I cued him again. Had the man been this forgetful in life?

"With Lorna, and I thought I would scope out the land. We Hipperty's are nothing if not diligent, you'll have heard about our diligence, no doubt."

"Of course. So you got to the top of the hill to have a look at the property, and then what?"

"And then nothing. It were night time and then you bleeders were carrying me back down here dressed in this." He gestured to the sparkling white dress he wore.

"Anyway, I've talked enough. This is the worst lock-in I've ever been to. Why doesn't someone pour me a pint? I'll have a Theakston's Black Bull Bitter please."

I looked at his tiny form. "I'm not sure that is a great idea. You're only borrowing this body." I didn't think Esmy's delicate frame was designed to cope with a Yorkshireman's appetite for ale.

"Don't be daft lad. I've been drinking pints since before I could spell 'em. I'd pour it myself if I wasn't suddenly so small. I can't reach the taps. Get on with it."

"Can you just give us a moment?" I gestured for Bella and Lupin to join me in the corner.

"What are we going to do?" I hissed.

"Well," said Lupin. "Looks like we will have to investigate old Mr Fairchild and his deadly cream buns. And if while we're doing it we happen to find out his secret recipe, well then, so much the better."

"Yes, obviously we are going to have to talk to him, but what should we do about Esmy the fairy girl? Her family are not going to be pleased that we've got her possessed by a racist, drunken, philandering property developer. We really don't want to get on the wrong side of the fairy folk. I once knew a chap who they cursed with seven years of hiccups just for stealing one of their chickens, think what they will do when they see what has happened to their daughter. Bella, tell me, where has the real Esmy gone and how do we get Mr Hipperty's ghost out of her?"

"I have no idea," said Bella.

As if to illustrate our plight there was a loud hiccup from the other side of the bar. The tiny fairy child was standing on a stool drinking Demon's Breath Porter from the tap.

"Right," I said. "We are in over our heads. We need someone who really knows about magic."

"I know about magic!" said Bella, indignantly.

"We need a witch." I replied. "We have to ask Lorna Brimtide."

As DAWN BROKE from behind Beech Ridge I stood with the heavy leopard's head knocker once more poised above the door to Pentdown Hall. It was orders of magnitude more impolite to call one's boss at half-past four in the morning than it was to disturb them at midnight. It would be awkward, embarrassing and not a little dangerous. But there was no other option. The fairy folk would have discovered Esmy's absence by now. The situation was beyond our control and we needed the input of a real witch, even if she might be a murderer.

Lorna took longer to come to the door this time, and when she did she looked sleepier, her hair was dishevelled and it was evident that we had got her from her bed. I held my breath, waiting to see how she would react, telling myself over and over that it was better to annoy a witch than it was to annoy the fairy folk. I wasn't sure I believed it.

"Mr Oak," she said. "I know I said I would always be here, but I'm not sure I quite expected you to call on me at this time. Was this how you behaved with my grandfather? I suspect not. What time is it by the way?"

"Half past four in the morning, and I'm really sorry Lorna. I wouldn't have come if it wasn't an emergency."

Her large eyes took in Bella and Lupin. "And you've bought some friends. The landlords. Have you all come from the pub?"

"Well, yes we have. But it's not like that at all. We haven't been drinking."

As if to make me look a liar the fairy gave a beery hiccup from the wheelbarrow in which we had pushed it, near comatose, up the hill. Lorna crouched next to the tiny figure.

"You bought a fairy with you, gosh I haven't met one of the Fae in years. And what's your name little fairy?" she said in the saccharine voice one uses on dim children who try their best.

"Geoffrey. Geoffrey Hipperty, and I ain't no blooming fairy, love," burped Esmy.

Lorna recoiled from the boozy breath and stood up. "Ah, I see. I think you might have a little problem here Albertus. Why don't you all come inside and tell me about it?"

WE SAT on Lorna's sofas, listening to the snores of the fairy while the day grew lighter outside. "So?" I asked, after explaining to the best of my abilities what had happened up on Beech Ridge. "How do we get Esmy back?"

"Well it's less a question of getting Esmy back and more a question of getting Mr Hipperty out," said Lorna.

"And how do we do that?"

"Well, first we can be glad she's not possessed by a demon, at least I don't think she is, I've never met a demon that called itself Geoffrey. A fairy possessed by a demon, now that's something that doesn't bear thinking about." She took a sip of her camomile tea and continued. "If what you suspect about Mr Hipperty's unfortunate demise is true then I think we can be pretty sure we are dealing with a ghost. His ghost to be precise. The ghost of Geoffrey Hipperty thinks it has unfinished business here in the physical world. Bella, you gave him force with your séance and he darted into the nearest unprotected body, the fairy child who had followed you up the hill. The only way to get him out is to finish whatever it is he thinks he has left to do here and let him go back to whatever realm it is that ghosts inhabit."

"What business do we have to finish for him? He was here looking for totty and I'm not helping with that." said Bella, miserably.

"Totty was his side mission," said Lupin. "He was here to do a property deal. We are going to have to buy him a field."

"I don't mean business literally, you're not going to have to build a housing estate" said Lorna. "I think that to avoid the wrath of the Fae you are going to have to find out just who it was that killed him, and you're going to have to do it quickly."

8

I woke from strange dreams of cream buns and elf violet with the midday light streaming through my windows. I had left Pentdown Hall at six in the morning with the sun up and birds singing in the hedgerows. Geoffrey had been in the middle of a long slurred rant about county cricket and I had sensed there would be no further revelations until she, or he, or whatever it was, sobered up. Lorna agreed and said she would be the childminder.

I stepped from my cottage into the herb garden, wondering if Lorna could legally sell my spirit tree to a dead man. She was insisting on holding her property development meeting with Geoffrey Hipperty, ostensibly in case the purchase of the bottom meadow really was his unfinished business. It was a worry. If he still remembered the name of his favourite beer, well, then there was no reason that he couldn't manage his old signature. Lorna might be helping us from compassion, but she could equally be looking to get the deeds exchanged before the spirit that possessed Esmy returned to the plains beyond.

My worries were mounting. What I most lacked were facts; facts about who the poisoner was, about who had sat in the beech tree, about why the fairies were in Whittleshin and facts about Lorna Brimtide's past and motives. Most of all I needed facts about what had happened between Geoffrey Hipperty buying his cream bun and ending up dead against the fence post. For this there could only be one witness, and I needed them as sober and clear headed as possible. I decided to make a herbal hangover cure and take it up to the big house.

To most people the small square outside my front door looked like botanical chaos, a riot of nonsensical colours and jumbled textures, but to me it made perfect sense. Everything was in its place for a reason. The things I used most often were closest to the front door, so if I was in the middle of simmering a stew I could run out and grab a handful of herbs. Other plants were grouped by use, so that if I needed to make one particular remedy I could find all the ingredients at once. My hangover patch was in the corner furthest from the door, because exercise is good for self-inflicted headaches, and from it I was able to gather a basket of milk thistle, thyme, peppermint, evening primrose and fennel seed.

I had developed this recipe one Christmas a few years earlier when Lupin had miscalculated the amount of sherry in his champagne trifle. The key ingredient was salicylic acid, so next I headed to the hedge of coppiced willow and shaved a sliver of fresh bark from that year's growth. I always kept my secateurs razor sharp in a holster on my hip, and I doubted that the willow even felt me whip away a strip of its protective outer skin, but I mind melded with it and apologised. It was the polite thing to do.

"No bother at all. I hardly noticed. Much more betterer things going on today than hungover dryads!" replied the willow.

I didn't pay the coppiced shrub much attention, willows were notoriously excitable, they thought rain was remarkable and noteworthy, and sun, and wind, and even light drizzle; talking to them could be like watching fifteen plays all at once. "It's not me that's hungover this time, actually," I melded back.

I made my way into the cottage and placed the herbs and bark in my blender with a bit of lime juice. Once whizzed together it looked like farmers' slurry and I'm sure it tasted similar, but no gain without pain. I poured it into a thermos flask and left once more for Pentdown Hall.

The garden seemed more than usually alive. I could make out the excited chatter of the borders and shrubs as a hum in the back of my brain. Plants talk to each other all the time, but it's usually not worth eavesdropping on. They go on about who was visited by a particularly flirtatious bee, or which of their neighbours has had his buds munched off by a hungry slug. Today was different. The lawns crackled with an energy I had not felt since the last time I accidentally over fertilised them, and even the hedges seemed to be abuzz. I stopped by a hawthorn, a reliable kind of plant, and asked it what on earth was going on.

It sounded dismissive and aloof. "Oh, everyone is excited about a murder," it drawled.

I wondered how word had got down from Beech Ridge about Geoffrey Hipperty's death. Beech trees rarely gossiped because none of the other plants enjoyed talking to them.

"Yes," I said. "He was looking down at my spirit tree from up on the ridge when he died."

"No he wasn't." Hawthorns have a reputation for being know-it-alls, but this was a bit much.

"Yes he was," I said. "I found him. Now if you'll excuse me I have to get on."

"Couldn't have been looking at your tree. They say this one is dead in a ditch. Only view is of mud."

The horrible possibility that there might be another body rose from my boots to my heart like blood poisoning. "What ditch? Where?" I asked.

"Don't know, just in a ditch. Better to ask the grass. Grass told me."

I groaned. There was nothing worse than trying to communicate with grass. It had an attention span of about two seconds, and its short term memory was not much better.

"Thank you," I told the hawthorn. I bent down to talk to the tawny summer grass that wove and flopped around the base of the hedge. The air was abuzz with chatter as I tuned into the grasses' conversation. I hit upon a patch of confused noise, like the static hiss of a detuned radio. The individual voices were hard to pick out, but now and then one blade would rise above the others. "A body!"

"The ditch!"

"It's dead!"

"A bee!"

I tried to get more details out of them; to the grass a

badger killed by a car would provoke the same reaction as a murdered human. I couldn't yet be sure that there had been another murder.

"Where is the body?" I questioned. "How big is it?"

"Big."

"In the ditch!"

"A body."

"A bee!"

It was no use. Grass communicated with its neighbours in a constant game of Chinese whispers, there was no telling where the rumour of the body started. Every clump had heard it from a thousand different directions and passed it on to a thousand more.

"It's dead."

"A body. In the ditch."

"A dead one."

"A murder!"

"A bee!"

9

The grass had unsettled me. It was like the cute child in a ghost story who starts talking his invisible friend. Innocent little plants should not talk about death and bodies. After making the Geoffrey Hipperty drink the disgusting herbal concoction, I took Lorna aside and explained what I had picked up from the plants in the garden. I told her I was sure it would be some roadkill, but I would have to go and look. She did not seem surprised by another potential murder, but then she had come down from London where murdering was more popular. It might be that she was doing her bit to introduce the pastime to us yokels.

I carried a stout pole of ash wood and wore my customary walking hat, determined that if anyone should see me they would think I was out on a casual stroll through the lanes, not searching for a potential murder victim. I started towards Wittleshin, trying to look as natural as possible, though my eyes darted around like fish in a millpond. I was just passing the first few cottages when I heard a disastrous noise:

"Albertus love, what a pleasant surprise. Have you come to see me about those daffodils?"

I winced at the high pitched call. I had forgotten my promise to see Felicity Jenkins about her troubling bulbs. From the exited tone it was clear that she had remembered, and had been waiting.

"I'm afraid I haven't Mrs Jenkins. I'm just off for a walk."

"Oh how lovely, and you've got the perfect day for it." She looked up at the bright blue summer sky. "You know it really is the biggest coincidence, but I was just about to head out for a walk myself. Tell you what Albertus, hang on a moment and I'll come with you."

She turned around and disappeared into her thatched cottage while I dithered outside the front gate. Philip Marlowe wouldn't have allowed his investigations to be compromised in such a manner. He would have told her 'Sorry doll, this is no walk for a dame.' And strode away. But I was no Philip Marlowe, and this was Wittleshin, not downtown Los Angeles, so I shuffled my feet at the gate, hoping that I could shake her off in the lanes somewhere.

Felicity's blond-haired head appeared from one of the downstairs windows. "Sorry Albertus love," she called. "Won't be a second, I'm just waiting for the kettle to boil, I thought we could take a thermos with us."

I wanted to tell her that homicide investigators didn't carry flasks of warm tea with them, they drank black coffee and smoked unfiltered cigarettes, but I thought better of it and instead shouted back: "Oh, thanks. Some tea would be lovely."

I considered informing her that this was not the average midmorning stroll, that it was in fact part of an ongoing investigation into a potential serial killer, but bit my tongue. The confession would only lead to awkward questions like: 'how do you know that,' and those would engender even more awkward answers like, 'a little clump of grass under the hedgerow told me.' I preferred that only the other supernaturally inclined residents of Wittleshin, like Bella, Lupin and now Lorna, knew about my strange talents. If I told the loud-mouthed divorcée I could talk with plants word would be around the village that I was stark raving mad. It would most likely lead to me being sectioned. If we found the body it would have to look like an unlucky accident.

Felicity emerged from the house, resplendent in a trademark tight blouse, this one in red polka-dots, and green wellington boots. She carried a high end pair of Kevlar walking poles and wore a small backpack that no doubt contained the thermos of tea and a quickly rustled-up picnic lunch.

"Righty ho then! Where are we going?" She bellowed, cheerfully.

Most walkers have a destination in mind, some notable wood, a hill with a spectacular view or an impressive stone. At the very least they have a convenient circuit that takes the stroller back to their starting place with the minimum of repetition. I would just be tramping back and forth along the lanes staring into ditches.

"It will not be the most exciting walk, I'm afraid. You

see, I'm..." I stuttered to a halt, looking for an explanation. "...I'm going to be hunting for mushrooms!"

"Oh how wonderful! I've always wanted to be taught how to forage like a real country person. What mushrooms are we going to be hunting for?" said Mrs Jenkins, enthusiastically. "I thought mushrooms only came out in the autumn."

"Most of them do, but there are some that come out in summer. We're looking for a very particular type of mushroom. It's called the ditch mushroom."

"The ditch mushroom? I've never heard of it. That doesn't sound very delicious to me."

"Well, it is. It's well worth spending all afternoon looking for, and maybe the evening. But it's very rare and it only grows in ditches so I'll need to trek the lanes carefully and keep my eyes on the ground."

As lies go it wasn't the best, but it would do.

WERE I less preoccupied with thoughts of death and murder it would have been a pleasant walk. The sun was shining and the hedgerows thrummed with life and activity. Mrs Jenkins kept up a constant cheerful patter, ranging from her ex-husband, through a dancing program on television, to the Women's Institute summer party she had been roped into organising. If I tuned out the words it was almost like the cheerful chatter of a half tamed songbird. She also kept us supplied with hot tea and sausage rolls, which were delicious but hard to swallow in my state of nervous agitation.

"As I was saying Albertus, you have to come along to

the W.I. summer party this Saturday. I have the biggest surprise planned for the baking competition. All those old ladies think that they have it sewn up, just because they've been baking the same dry old Victoria sponge since the last Ice Age, but I'm going to show them! I've bought myself a special cake measuring ruler, mine are going to be millimetre perfect. I don't think even Mr Fairchild's cream buns will be in with a chance this year."

"Mmmhmm," I mumbled, noncommittally.

"I saw your new boss yesterday, walking past the house. A silk dress, in Whittleshin? She looks very full of herself, if you ask me." I hadn't asked, and I detected a jealous undertone to her words. "I don't think that's her real hair colour, I'm certain she dyes it. What do you think Albertus?"

"I really couldn't tell you, I hardly know the woman," I said, as we headed out of the village on a lane that generations of feet, hooves and cartwheels had sunk into the soil.

I kept up the pretence that I was looking for mushrooms, which was doubly deceptive because had we really been going mushroom hunting there was no way I would have taken another person with me. The fertile fungal beds of Wittleshin were a well guarded secret amongst the foraging community. Every autumn when the chanterelles were in season myself and Lupin would engage in elaborate subterfuge to find each other's favourite hunting grounds. He liked to dry and pulverise the delicate yellow chanterelles and use them as an enriching agent for the Bull and Firkin's earthy game sauces; I preferred the trumpets sautéed in butter and slapped on toast as a warming breakfast when the days were getting colder. Just thinking about their complex flavour set my mouth salivating. I wondered if the beeches up on the ridge were so unfriendly because they really were harbouring truffles, perhaps I ought to get myself a truffle pig.

"So what do ditch mushrooms look like?" asked Mrs Jenkins, wrenching me from my dreams of autumn flavours.

"Oh, you'll know when you see them, they're sort of mushroomy and ditch-bound."

"Can you use them to make risotto?"

"Yes," I lied, confidently this time. I was getting better at it. "They work wonderfully in Italian cuisine. The trick is to use a little of the ditch water as a stock."

"Well then Albertus, once we have found some I'd like you to let me cook you a nice risotto. You can come round to mine. We will have a glass of wine in the garden. It can be my thank you for teaching me how to gather ditch mushrooms."

It was wrong to deceive Felicity, but I knew there was no chance of finding any of the fictitious crop, so I enthusiastically agreed to her proposal.

We carried on at a steady pace through a maze of winding paths and ancient lanes, scanning the ground for anything that may have excited the grass. I focused on one side of the lane, Felicity the other, and we progressed leisurely, that was, until she startled me with a scream.

"Oh, Albertus how horrible, I think it's dead." The dreaded moment had arrived. I crossed over to her side of the lane and there in the ditch lay a small muntjac deer on a flattened piece of grass. A car had obviously clipped it the night before.

"Oh good, that's fantastic. What a relief," I said, happy that I wasn't looking at another human victim.

Felicity Jenkins turned to me angrily, her love for all God's creatures burning in her eyes. "How can you possibly say that?"

"Oh no, I'm not happy it's dead." I genuinely wasn't, despite the damage the blighters did in the garden, nibbling the bark from my trees and saplings with their sharp little teeth. "I just mean that it could have been far worse, that's all."

"How could it have been worse? It's dead, Albertus."

"Well... it died quickly and at least the car didn't swerve to avoid it and end up crashing through the hedge and killing a cow. Things could have been a lot worse here and we should both be very thankful. But don't worry Felicity, I'll come back with one of my spades and bury it straightaway."

I began to stride off towards Pentdown Hall.

"Wait, Albertus! We haven't found any ditch mushrooms yet! Are you giving up? What about my risotto?"

"I just don't think there's going to be any mushrooms Felicity, maybe the weather has been a little dry recently. We're not going to find any so let's get back to the village."

Felicity seemed disappointed but she came along with me. We walked silently through the shaded lane until she tugged on my sleeve. "Albertus, look! Ditch mushrooms!"

I followed the line of her outstretched finger to the bottom of the roadside ditch where a perfect circle of white-capped, dark-stemmed mushrooms was growing.

"Shall we pick them?" She said, excitedly.

"No, those are not ditch mushrooms," I said, trying to keep the alarm from my voice.

"Well, they are growing in a ditch, and they are certainly mushrooms. They look like ditch mushrooms to me. How can you be sure they are not?"

"I just know, okay?" I said, sounding like I was talking to a small child, but judging it better to patronise her than explain my certainty — we were looking at a fairy ring. The perfect circle of fungal growth left where the fairy folk had been working their earth magic. I wondered what the Fae had been doing in a ditch so far away from their encampment, and what spell it was they had cast.

"How do they grow in such a perfect circle?" asked Felicity. "Oh look, there's another one further up." She walked on down the lane. "And another one over there. There are even more of them up there, growing all around that thing in the ditch."

"What thing?" I followed her eyes to where a lumpy form lay in a pool of shallow water. A large bulky shape that appeared to be wearing hiking boots.

All the colour had drained from Mrs Jenkins face. She had worked out what it was at the same time as me. "Do you have your phone?" I asked her.

She nodded dumbly, the first time I had known her unable to speak. She pulled out the telephone and muttered: "no signal."

"Then go back to the village, quickly! I'll stay here with the body. Find someone with a phone and call the police."

She rushed back in the direction we had come and I stooped to examine the ditch. Besides the body there was nothing in the trench but a single piece of paper, which I scooped up and placed in my pocket.

Whoever lay there was tall, bulky and very dead. Their trousers seemed to be sprinkled with white powder. I felt for a pulse but the cold the flesh told there was no chance of resuscitation. It was an effort to turn, but with a slurp the mud released its grip and the body rolled onto its back. I was staring down at the moustachioed and bright blue face of Mr Fairchild the baker.

10

"There he was, dead in his hiking boots." I said.

"And the police are saying it's another heart attack?" said Lorna, incredulously. She took a sip of her Drover's Delight which was a little too hoppy for my tastes, but still a good session ale. "What's wrong with those bumpkins?"

I shook my head. Yes, the Wittleshin police force were slow, and yes Inspector Davies was a vain and incompetent idiot, but they were our police force and the provincial villager in me bristled to hear a Londoner come down and criticise them. She'd start talking about house prices next, laughing greedily when she found out how many of our little ramshackle cottages she could buy for the price of a Zone Two flat. "I don't know that there's anything wrong with them," I said. "Remember they have no idea elf violet exists. A big man like him, out for a strenuous walk on a hot day. The police know that Fairchild's diet was almost entirely sugar and jam and that his one hobby was getting blood boilingly angry customers and things he read in the newspaper. If I were investigating without knowing about elf violet it would seem pretty straightforward to me."

"He had more hobbies than that," said Lorna.

"I don't think he did."

"Well you found him out in the lanes in a pair of hiking boots. He must have enjoyed walking."

"He liked stamping. Stamping up to the fields and stamping back again. He said it was good practice for standing behind a counter all day. He once told me that you could tell the stamina of a baker by how far away you could hear him. He certainly was not a hard man to track." I took a sip of my beer and sat back in my chair.

"Oh, well that's interesting. I suppose that for you it's a jolly good job that the police don't know about elf violet," Lorna said.

"What do you mean?"

"Nothing...," she said. "...Well, I'm just saying. If they were treating this as a murder enquiry they would start looking for links. I know Inspector Davies is no Sherlock Holmes but even he might work out that having two bodies, both out in the middle of nowhere, and both found by the same person automatically makes the finder the prime suspect."

"If we're hunting for primes, Lorna Brimtide, I might remind you that I have lived in Wittleshin for over four hundred years, and in all that time I can count the number of suspicious deaths on my fingers. You have lived in Wittleshin for two days and there has been a murder on both of them."

"And I might remind you that you were the one who grew the elf violet. In this particular mystery my money is on the gardener."

From the other side of the table the tiny fairy girl gave a deep chuckle.

"Oh shut up," I snapped. "Mr Fairchild was surrounded by fairy rings. I'd suggest you people should be under just as much suspicion as me, probably more. This murder has all the marks of the Fae."

"My people? My people are the Hipperty's, and we have nothing to do with mushrooms, never had, never will. Spores and the like, I don't trust them. Anyway, your friend just spent most of this morning convincing me that I'm a ghost not a fairy. I'm the victim here so you can't pin this on me."

I conceded the point. "Have you remembered any more about that night yet?"

The fairy-ghost took a sip of his lemonade. "Not a jot," he said with a belch.

We were saved from further conversation by Lupin, who burst through the doors, his face flushed from the heat of the kitchen.

"Here we go," he said, cheerfully. "There's no crisis that couldn't be improved by fresh cooked Scotch eggs. I know a double homicide is more serious than Wittleshin's normal dramas, so I've made something special. Duck eggs with chorizo, black pudding and a sourdough crumb."

I lifted one of the crispy breaded eggs from the tray and bit into it. Under the meat the yolk of the duck egg was deliciously hot and liquid, a contender for yolk of the year, it mingled perfectly with the salty meat surrounding it. Every cloud has a silver lining and these bar snacks were ours. "Now, there's proper food!" trilled the fairy through a mouthful of egg.

"Where is Bella?" Asked Lorna, her mouth only slightly less full.

"I don't know," Lupin replied, his words muffled by the food. "I thought I saw her talking to Mrs Dobson out on the village green an hour ago, maybe she's finally been persuaded to join the Women's Institute. I warn you though Bertie, she is not happy that you dragged her back here on her day off."

As if obeying a theatrical cue Bella entered, her face furrowed and her brow like thunder. She looked straight at me.

"This better be good Albertus, I had a date tonight, with a doctor, a real doctor this time, he sent me a picture of his stethoscope to prove it." Bella had been conned by philosophy PhD's calling themselves doctors before. In the seas of online dating it seemed that there were more sharks than fishermen. "And then you make me come back here, which leaves me stuck talking to that crazy old lady for goodness knows how long."

"Oh yes, how is Mrs Dobson?" said Lupin.

"Honestly I have never heard such a load of hot air! She was going on about her toilet, apparently it's making a squeaking noise, so I gave her Steve the Plumber's number and thought that would shut her up, but no! Look at this. She's given me a hundred posters to put up around the village, and there's only forty telegraph poles in the whole of Wittleshin! I ended up agreeing to go to her stupid summer party just to get her to stop talking to me." The words fell from her mouth in an uninterrupted rush, the end of each sentence joining the next as if welded together. You had to be a serious talker to stop Bella getting a word in edgeways. Mrs Dobson deserved a medal.

"Lupin, you'll come with me, won't you? I'm going to need you there for moral support, you could enter the cake baking competition! The look on all their faces when you beat them! You must come with me!"

"I don't think I can Bella," said Lupin.

"Of course you can, if I'm going then you're going too. It's the brotherly thing to do. Someone else can look after the kitchen while you're gone, it will only be for a few hours."

"No Bella, I really don't think I can come. It's..." He dropped his voice. "It's that time of the month."

Lorna looked at him quizzically, Mr Hipperty the fairy burst out laughing.

"I think it's probably okay to tell them," I said.

Lupin glared at Geoffrey. "Not that time of the month," he growled. "Wolf time of the month, the night where if I'm not tied up securely I head out and eat tasty little morsels like you."

Geoffrey continued to snigger. "Already dead lad, remember?" he said.

"It's a full moon in two days' time?" asked Lorna.

"Sure is," said Lupin. "Why?"

"Nothing, it's just that it's also the summer solstice in two days. It's not often the two combine. The night is going to be awfully heavy with magic."

I decided that the time had come to tell the Lestrades what Lorna and Mr Hipperty already knew. I cleared my throat but my audience continued to chatter excitedly amongst themselves. The tap of my fork against half empty glass did nothing to quell their rhubarbing. "Everybody quiet!" I shouted.

The four of them froze, Bella's mouth open, Mr Hipperty's tiny pale hands reaching out for Lupin's unguarded pint of beer.

"There's been another murder," I told them.

"How do you know?" asked Bella.

"I found the body."

My audience were shocked into silence, eventually Bella managed to speak. "Again?"

"Yes, again."

"Is it…"

"Elf-violet? I think so. His face was bright blue. It was Mr Fairchild."

The Lestrade siblings had been operating alongside the bakery for years, and despite the proprietor's irascible nature they had a strong neighbourly relationship. "No," muttered Bella. "Kill Geoffrey, fine. Mr Fairchild was one of us!"

"Mr Fairchild," chuckled Geoffrey. "The miserable sod who sold me my last cream bun? What's next for the Famous Five? That gets rid of your only suspect, doesn't it?"

"I don't know about that, if anything it makes it more likely he was involved. Maybe he was working with someone and they decided he knew too much and bumped him off," volunteered Lorna.

I wanted to be sensitive to Lupin and Bella, but realised that if there was a serial killer stalking Wittleshin we didn't have time for niceties. We needed to get straight to the heart of the problem.

"Perhaps he wasn't bumped off, perhaps it was an accident. We already suspect he had elf violet on his property, perhaps it got mixed with something. Or perhaps he was overcome with guilt about what happened to Mr Hipperty, perhaps…"

"…he did it to himself?" interrupted Bella. "No, not Mr Fairchild. He gave the impression of being as miserable as sin, but we knew him, he just wasn't the type to do that. He had the Women's institute baking contest to win."

"Do you think it could have been one of the other bakers? Someone else who wanted to win the Women's Institute contest? One of your old gas bags, Bella? Mrs Dobson?" said Lorna.

Bella looked angry. "I know we might seem petty and trivial to you big city witches but I can promise that even Mrs Dobson wouldn't murder someone over a cake competition. And what about you, Geoffrey? Were you planning to submit a sponge cake?"

"Was I heck!" said the fairy.

"We have to get into the bakery. There's just a small wall between our service yard and his, we could easily break a window. Maybe there is a clue in there somewhere," said Lupin, already starting to stand and head for the door. He became a trifle gung-ho as the full moon approached.

"Wait Lupin! Before we start breaking and entering there's another group we need to look into," I said. I quickly told them of the circles of crooked-stemmed mushrooms I had found all along the bottom of the ditch.

"Fairy magic!" exclaimed Lorna. "People only started getting killed when the fairies arrived in the village. It must be them!"

"You arrived at the same time," said Bella before I kicked her under the table. I hadn't got to the bottom of the mysterious city-witch, but there was a possibility we might need her magic at some point and I was keen to keep her on our side.

"I also found this." I pulled the crumpled piece of paper from my pocket. It was sodden with ditch water and on the verge of falling apart, but blue markings were visible on its surface, cryptic runes and squiggles written in ballpoint pen.

"It's the same language as before," said Bella.

"Something weird is going on here. Did you talk to the Mushrooms?" Asked Lupin. "Do your funny mind-meld trick on them?" He was struggling to sit still.

I shook my head. "Mushrooms are not part of the plant kingdom. I don't have the ability to communicate with fungus, you need a bogeyman for that. Besides, these were of the magical world, not the natural. I doubt they would have wanted to talk with me."

"So, maybe I should go and have a word with the fairies, see what they know?" asked Lupin.

Despite his shock at Fairchild's death he was enjoying his role as an amateur sleuth. The cooking detective, ready to investigate any crime, as long as it wasn't dark outside. I thought of the Fae I had met on the night of the first murder. Then they had been wary and hostile out of habit, now they had justified cause for anger and paranoia. Approaching them would be last thing Lupin did in three dimensions. There would be a caravan rolling out of Wittleshin with a new painting of a big, friendly dog on the side.

"It won't work," I said. "The Fae would never talk. The only way we could find out what was going on and why they are here is if we had one of them, one of the Fae, on our side. An informer."

"Oh, no lads. No. Nope, nope, no!" said Mr Hipperty. "Don't you look at me like that, I'm not doing it. Nope."

"Not like that Geoffrey. You sound like a bad drag queen. *You have to speak like this,*" said Lorna, doing a very passable impression of the fairy folk's tinkling vocal tones.

"*I 'ave to speak like this,*" said Geoffrey, sounding like the ghost of a Yorkshire property developer.

"Like *this,*" said Lorna, her voice trilling.

"Like *this,*" echoed Geoffrey.

"That's it! Nearly there," said Lorna, excitedly. I suppose it made sense that Geoffrey could speak like Esmy, after all it was her body he was possessing, he was using her vocal chords.

Bella had the same idea. "Geoffrey, you need to relax, suppress your ego. Let go of everything that you think makes you who you are and give in to your body."

"What a load of hippy clap-trap," said Geoffrey, more dour than ever. "Can't abide hippies. Worse than Londoners, they are. Or nearly worse."

"Come on, I'll give you a massage," said Bella. "Help you relax into yourself."

"Now you're talking lass!"

Bella laid her hands on the tiny fairy's shoulders and began to work them with the balls of her thumbs. After a while she started to hum to herself, still working Geoffrey's shoulders. She spoke quietly, whispered words that seemed to be some sort of chant. I could only catch fragments and snatches of what she was saying, phrases like, "floating away" and "let go of the self." Geoffrey seemed to be drifting towards sleep, his eyelids slipping down to obscure his silver irises.

The rest of us said nothing while Bella worked. Eventually the enchantress spoke in her normal voice.

"How do you feel Geoffrey?" she asked.

"Fine," said Geoffrey, abruptly. The rest of us froze, his voice was high and crystalline, like the tinkling of a thousand silver-bells.

"Bloody hell," exclaimed Geoffrey, angelically.

"Well done, Bella!" Lupin gave his sister an enthusiastic bear-hug.

"Great work. Now we just have to think how you will explain where you have been for the last few days," I said.

"Oh, I wouldn't worry too much about that," said Lorna. "The Fae have a different attitude towards parenting to overprotective human types. They probably haven't even noticed that Esmy has gone. If they ask anything Geoffrey can just tell them that he got into a conversation with the hills, or he was debating a riddle with the river. They love all that kind of stuff. I was catching moon beams in a spiderweb net..."

"I'll blag it," said Geoffrey. "I was Harrogate poker

champion 1998 and 2003. My bluffing is impeccable. Trick is to look out for the tiniest tells on your opponent's face without giving away a single clue about your own thoughts. My poker-face is inscrutable. I am in-scroot-able, I tell you."

For all our sakes I hoped his confidence was well founded.

11

In a gardener optimism is deadly. It kills plants. A horticulturist with a half-full glass will send his flowers to die in the frosty trenches. If one values survival one urges restraint, one urges prudence, and above all, one urges pessimism. But faint heart never won fair praise, and I am a gardener of the bright side. Yes, I have witnessed sights that will haunt me until I fall. I have seen ribbons of *Eucomis comosa* turn black under October skies. I have seen grafts fail, cuttings wither and bulbs blasted into black mush. But for the beauty I have created I would kill them all over again.

Without optimism I would have never created an entirely new style of gardening at Pentdown Hall, one that has since spread to forward thinking gardens across the country: The English Stately Jungle. The movement's key feature is pairing ancient buildings with outrageous tropical plantings. They use it to great effect in Oxford, where one can look out of medieval mullioned windows and, beyond the perfect lawns, see a great leafy wall of ricinus, tetrapanax and colocasia. I have slightly gone off the look myself, and the walls at Pentdown are again hung with swags of sweet-smelling roses, but my goodness, those years when the red sails of the Abyssinian banana ruled this English valley will never be forgotten. All of it came from throwing caution to the wind and expecting the best.

Which is a long winded way of saying I was trying to keeps my hopes up. Perhaps our plan would work. Against all odds Geoffrey would skip back and tell us who had killed him and the baker, and why. But as I wandered around the garden, inefficiently dead-heading astrantia and aquilegia, I found more negative scenarios to picture than positive. I would happily face the wrath of the fairies, but if the truth of Esmy's possession came out Bella and Lupin would also be dragged into things. I should have left them in the pub that night and trekked up to Beech Ridge alone.

In the Monstrous Glade I sat down on a mossy stone bench and rested my chin on my fist. Here in the shade of grotesque and looming evergreens the air was cool and neutral. It was a relief to get away from the perfume and light of the herbaceous gardens. The area had once been a fussy little avenue, a Dutch style promenade where ladies could walk past dainty little topiary spirals and marvel at man's command over nature. Then Patience Brimtide had died and her husband had locked himself in the model dairy for fifteen years and I had let the plants grow wild. Old Henry Brimtide had eventually emerged from the dairy, dusted down his jacket and breeches and returned to London to take up his seat in parliament. He never returned to Pentdown Hall, and none of the Brimtides who had inhabited it since had ever mentioned the prim little yews. For hundreds of years I had been shaping them into vast craggy shapes. They hulked and hunkered down over the garden visitor, their sides bulging out like bubbling plastic in a house fire. All of them were mad, driven crazy by the decades of constraint and their subsequent release. I had given up trying to communicate with them, they told stories of ancient sleeping gods, of a tentacled giant that lay beneath the Cotswolds and a race of liquid things that lived behind a tear in reality. I was getting just about desperate enough to ask them what to do when a friendly voice rescued me.

"Hello Albertus. I brought you a cup of tea."

I looked up to see Lorna crossing the lawn carrying two mugs. Her normally immaculate hair was dishevelled. A blue smear ran down one side of her face.

"I'm afraid it's slightly cold. It took a while to find you. I've never been to this part of the garden." She looked up at the bulging cliff of yew needles. "There's a strange atmosphere here. Is this where you come to get away from things?"

I took a sip of tea. "Not really. I don't know why I'm here, it just seemed the right place. If I'm honest with you Lorna, I don't normally need to get away from things. Normally gardening and a good lunch are enough to cure me of my worries."

"I feel the same. I've been trying to focus on my work but all my potions are exploding and the perfumes smell like this." She held out her wrist. It was very pale and smelled like a synthetic banana. "That's not going to sell to the ladies that lunch, is it?"

I shook my head.

"Why do you care?" Lorna asked.

"What do you mean?"

"Judging by your spirit tree you've seen the village die ten times over already. People come, people go, you stay in the meadow. Does it really matter if someone takes their bow little earlier than they might have done?"

"They're all compost anyway?"

"Exactly."

"You're right. That's the way of the tree. And I've lived like that. I've dug thirty Brimtide graves in your family burial ground with my eyes dry. But I like these villagers. Even when they won't let me walk to the pub with out bothering me and when they make me judge their silly flower shows. Maybe the people have changed, maybe I have, but this lot, Bella and Lupin and all the others, they're not disposable, they're my friends."

Lorna put her hand on my shoulder. "Does that mean you won't have dry eyes when you dig my grave?" She laughed.

"Something tells me I won't be burying you." I said, or started to say. We were interrupted by the northern fairy before I could finish.

"Ey up love birds! Hiding in the shrubbery, eh? Well, look lively, I've got some news for you." From the sounds of it Geoffrey was still squatting in Esmy's body. It could only be good news. If they had suspected they were harbouring one of the Harrogate Hippertys the fairies would surely not have let it leave. That was, unless we were now dealing with a double agent.

"So?" asked Lorna. "How was it? I told you they wouldn't even notice that Esmy was gone." The concern had fallen from her voice. It sounded as if she was about to laugh.

"Nope. They noticed all right. Not quite so clever as you thought after all." The fairy still spoke in the high pitched voice natural to its body, but after a couple of seconds of vigorous coughing and grunting managed to inhabit the tones of the gruff property developer. "In fact they had been searching for me. Well not for me, for Esmy. You know what I mean?"

"What did you tell them?" I asked.

"Well I told them I'd been yacking away with a hill and completely lost track of the time."

"And did they believe you?"

"Did they Heck! They locked me in one of the caravans. But it had thin walls, so I was able to get an idea of what was going on. I always thought I'd make a good spy me, ears like a hawk."

"And..." I prompted.

"Oh they were all spouting a load of nonsense about a growing evil, dark forces, that sort of clap trap. If I'm honest I gave up listening after a while. Geoffrey Hipperty has no time for mumbo jumbo."

Lorna was visibly annoyed. "Geoffrey you wretch. You're a blooming ghost, you live in the body of a fairy! How can you say you've no time for mumbo-jumbo? You're two-and-a-half feet of walking, talking mumbo!"

The tiny creature threw me an exaggerated wink and began to laugh. "Just messing with you. I heard enough. Basically, lads, I think we're in for more of the same. There is a lot of talk about prophesies, and dark powers, it seems to all be about the summer solstice. The fairies are here because apparently this place is on a load of ley lines, hey maybe that's why the property prices are so messed up! It's not just them who are here. There is some magic spell, or ritual or something that can only be done in this place, at this time, this particular year, whoever carries it out gets to ask for their heart's one true desire. They've come along to see what happens. A load of bloomin' rubberneckers."

"Why were they in the ditch with Mr Fairchild's body?" I asked.

"I couldn't work that out. They know he's dead for sure though, they were talking about the second victim having been found already."

"But is it them? Did they do it?"

"I don't have a clue. But there is one more thing you should know. They seem certain that there will be another murder, and that it will be tonight."

12

"I'm telling you, Inspector Davies, there will be another murder and it will be tonight! You need to call for back-up, we need teams out, canine units, boots on the ground. You have to radio for a helicopter!"

The policeman slurped from his mug of instant coffee. He was stood in the control nexus of the Whittleshin Justice Machine — a small meeting room attached to the village hall. It was a space Davies' shared with folding chairs for the monthly film night and the toddler group's soft play equipment. On the floor someone had painted a lurid yellow stripe and a laminated sign on the wall warned of consequences for trespassing beyond it.

"Mr Oak, listen to yourself," said Davies. "You're saying the fairies told you that someone is going to die tonight. You're not making any sense. A nice cup of tea and a good night's sleep will sort all this out far better than a police helicopter. Because the way you're talking now, well, I'm starting to think you might be a danger to yourself and others." He gestured towards his handcuffs, put down his drink and laid a hand on my shoulder. "And I have a duty to protect."

I shrugged him away and slammed my fist down on the trestle table desk. I was getting frustrated and knew it was showing on my face. Davies looked at the floor. With out any authorisation I had crossed his yellow line. "No, you haven't been listening to me at all!" I shouted. "The fairies didn't tell me, they were overheard by the ghost they had imprisoned who then told me. I'm serious! Please Inspector Davies, they have already killed two people!" I tried to keep my voice steady. My words might be those of a lunatic but my delivery could still be that of a steady headed citizen.

"Mr Oak, I am a very patient man," Davis lied. "But you are really starting to test me. I know it must have been rough on you, finding both bodies like that, but it was just pure bad luck. Two heart attacks. The coroner told me so."

"They did not have heart attacks! They were poisoned!"

"Yes," said Inspector Davies sarcastically. "By elf violet, you already told me. And I told you that no such plant exists. It says so on Wikipedia," He picked up his phone and read from the screen. "Elf violet is a magical plant in British and Irish mythology." Davies sat back, folded his arms and smirked, as If I was supposed to be impressed by this evidence of an independent investigation. "So please leave me alone. I've given this ludicrous story enough of my time. If I have reasonable cause to suspect that you are a danger to yourself or anyone else then I have a duty to take you in to custody, for your own safety. I'll lock you ruddy well up Albertus! Now tell me again... what did the clump of grass tell you?"

It had been foolish to involve the police. They were under resourced and apathetic. Even searching for motives behind the scout hut graffiti had been a conjectural leap too far for poor Davies. It was almost cruel to burden him with talk of dark ceremonies and the summer solstice. He did not react well to well to uncertainties. For people like me the unknown is alluring, for him mysteries were frustrating and ultimately enraging. Like many people he clung to the delusion that the world was a simple. Anything that introduced nuance to his life threatened to raise suppressed fears that he might not know everything, and like any threatened creature he was liable to lash out. It would be almost impossible to stop the next murder from the comfort of a secure psychiatric unit.

"You are right Inspector. Maybe I am just tired. Perhaps I will go home to bed after all," I said.

Inspector Davies gave me a suspicious nod. "I think that might be wise Mr Oak. I'll drive you home." He reached for his car keys and the plastic handcuffs hanging beside them.

"No Inspector. Thank you very much but I think a bit of fresh air will do me good," I shouted over my shoulder as I walked from the police station.

Once outside I called Lorna. The line was bad and she was whispering, doing her best to remain unnoticed in the lookout position I had sent her to. "Yes, I can see them, I'm just outside the camp in a big bush. No one has left or arrived since I got here. If they are up to something they are being very discreet about it.

Someone is playing the fiddle and I think I can hear dancing."

"Okay, well if they make any movements call me, stay there all night if you have to. I'm going down to the Bull and Firkin to enlist the others. And Lorna, please be careful." I realised that my concern for the witch was genuine. I hardly knew her, she was a certified blackmailer and for all I knew a priestess of the dark arts, but I seemed to care for her. This was some powerful magic.

BELLA LOOKED ALARMED as I breathlessly burst into the pub. With my wild eyes and my dishevelled hair she was probably concerned I would scare the customers away.

"Bertie, are you okay, what's happened? I was so worried about you," she whispered, trying to keep her words inaudible to anyone but us.

"What are you talking about?" I replied.

"Inspector Davies just called. He asked if either of us had seen you this evening. He sounded very serious. We thought that maybe you'd been poisoned too." My friend was close to tears.

"No I'm fine. It's just that I tried to explain what had been happening and I think I may have come across as a little...mad."

Lupin came out of the kitchen, wiping his hands on a dish towel and stooping to avoid banging his head on the doorframe. "What's going on Bertie? I see you've not been poisoned, that's good news?"

"Shut up Lupin," snapped Bella. "He's told the police about the murders."

"Why did you tell them that? You said that there was no way they would ever believe you."

"They didn't believe me. But I was desperate! Geoffrey came back from the fairies. He thinks there will be another killing."

"Bloody hell. Do you think the Fae are behind this? And do you think they'll take requests?" said Lupin. His galling flippancy said more about the state of the moon than the seriousness of our situation.

"No, well, maybe, I don't think so." The words were coming out of my mouth faster than my tongue could flap. With the slurs and spittle I probably sounded as insane to Bella and Lupin as I had to Inspector Davies.

"Slow down," said Bella. "We can't help with this until we know everything you do. What exactly did Geoffrey say?"

I explained what had happened to Mr Hipperty's ghost, how he had been locked in the caravan and had overheard the fairies saying that there would be another murder.

"But how did Geoffrey get out to tell you? I thought he was banged up," said Lupin once I had finished my wild and breathless explanation. "Can we trust him?"

I realised that I had no idea how Geoffrey had managed to get out of his mobile prison. He hadn't told us that much.

"Albertus, Lupin's right. We don't know what his motives are," said Bella. "Do you think there is any possibility he might have been lying to you? He was very proud of his bluffing," she continued. "He might not even have gone to see the Fae. Or maybe he did, and he's working as a double agent. As Lupin says, how did he get out?"

I was growing frustrated with this line of enquiry. "Maybe he was, maybe he wasn't! We can't take the risk of ignoring him. We have to get out there and stop it! Come on, bring flashlights and bring lots of tea!"

"Wait," commanded Bella. "If we all go out there and start charging around randomly the only thing that is going to happen is that we will all get ourselves sectioned. We need to know more. We have to at least have some idea where to look."

"She's right Bertie," said Lupin. "Hurtling around willy-nilly won't get us anywhere."

I looked from brother to sister. Both wore stern faces. I considered dashing back out to search the lanes alone but I knew I was acting hysterically. Lupin was on the verge of his transformation and even he could see that I was behaving like the mad-man Inspector Davies believed me to be. "You're right," I said, sitting down on a barstool. "So, what are we going to do?"

Lupin shrugged his big shoulders and made a 'beats me' kind of face. I looked at Bella imploringly. "Perhaps you could try the spirit world again?" I suggested. "They might tell us what's going on."

"Are you sure that's wise? After what happened last time..." said Bella.

"No! I'm not having you bring down spirits in here Bella. You are my sister and I love you dearly but there is no way I will let you curse this pub.

I stood up, desperate to reassure Lupin. "There's no danger of anything going wrong this time Lupin, I promise. Bella won't use a crystal ball, she'll use...?" I looked at Bella who shrugged her shoulders in response.

"...tea leaves?" I suggested.

Bella shook her head.

"Tarot cards?"

Another shake of the head.

"Magic eight ball?"

They laughed and I felt that I might win Lupin over. He had started to wear the rakish grin of the werewolf. "Bella is there anything at all you might be able to use, apart from your crystal ball? Something to get in touch with the spirit world."

She thought for a moment. "I suppose I could use the Ouija board."

I looked at Lupin imploringly. "Come on Lupin, what could go wrong with an Ouija board? This could be our only chance to stop somebody dying. Maybe another one of our neighbours, maybe one of the regulars. It doesn't matter if your souffles are haunted if there is no one left to eat them, does it now?"

I saw Lupin's resolve crumble. He was grinning with the adventure of it all. The advantage of years of friendship was that I knew what his weak spots were. I decided to press home my advantage. "Good lad. Now quickly, Bella, go and get the board, do you want us to light candles or anything like that?"

"Um I don't really think it matters," said Bella. "If it makes you feel in the mood then go for it. The key thing when using the board is that everyone taking part believes in its power."

～

A FEW MINUTES later the three of us were sitting in a triangle around one of the small pub tables. There was a worrying symmetry between our positions and those we had adopted up on Beech Ridge two nights before. This time there was no protective pentangle and no ring of soil to protect us from the world beyond the veil.

Lupin had shooed the drinkers out of the public bar and hung a sign on the door saying the Bull and Firkin was closed for a private function. The curtains were drawn to block out the light of the summer evening. This was not a time for disturbances. Our mobile phones were switched off and hidden in the beer cellar. There would be nothing to distract us from communication with the spirits.

In my limited experience people who used Ouija boards held their hands on top of a drinking glass, so I expected Bella to fetch a half pint tankard from behind the bar. Instead she produced a stone disk with a hole in the middle and laid it on the table in front of us. It was a smooth granite donut, the kind of object that called on you to pick it up and test its weight, feel its strange contours. Lupin and I were both instructed to place our index fingers on the odd circular counter. Bella did the same.

I shuddered as I touched the polished surface. The stone was cold, as if it had been stored in Lupin's walk-in freezer. I couldn't tell its colour. It seemed to change hue with whatever angle I viewed it from.

"So?" said Lupin. "What do we ask it?"

"Whatever you like," said Bella, not sounding confident in her answer.

"Hello, Ouija board. I'm Albertus, pleasure to meet

you. I was just wondering if you would answer a quick question for me? Will someone be murdered tonight?"

The stone started to move under our fingers. Although its surface was glassy the noise it made was harsh and grating, as though it were being dragged over a gravel drive. Perhaps Ouija boards were coated in sandpaper, perhaps we were hearing the rasp of whatever sat on the board's invisible dimension. I had asked a simple question but the counter avoided the sections marked 'yes' and 'no.' Instead it began to spell out a word, Lupin mouthed each letter out loud. "F. D. D. E. P. Z. U. J." The stone came to a stop.

"Fddepzuj. That's not a word," said Lupin. There was a mixture of relief and disappointment in his voice.

"No," admitted Bella. "No it is not. I think the problem is with the way you asked the question. You are not talking to the board Albertus, you are supposed to be using it as a conduit to get to the spirits beyond. Here, let me try." She adopted a voice an octave below her natural tones. "Oh! Great denizens of the spirit world. Mighty beings of the beyond. We call on you now in our hour of greatest need."

Lupin gave his sister a double thumbs up. She nodded at the table.

"Oh, right," said Lupin, putting his fingers back on the smooth stone disk.

Bella hammed on: "In your infinite wisdom please give us guidance in this our time of trial and tribulation. Blood has been spilled and but for you blood shall be spilled again!"

"No blood was spilled. It just went blue," said Lupin.

Bella glared at him and then back at the table. The

stone counter jagged around, not stopping over a letter
long enough for us to read it. The abrasive noise hacked
at my inner ears and it was all I could do to keep my
hands on the table. A. J. S. G. G. G. I started to get frustrated, we were wasting our time with a child's board
game when we could be out preventing a murder. My
plan of running about the lanes until I caught the killer
or was killed myself was looking attractive once more.

The atmosphere in the room changed. The candles
began to flicker and gutter out. The television hissed into
life and then died in static. The stone grew colder until
my fingers stuck to it.

"Is somebody there?" asked Bella. The stone slid sideways until we could read 'yes' through the hole in the
centre. "Will there be another murder tonight?"

The stone moved again. This time not in random
spirals but in a controlled glide. The three of us held our
breath and when Bella exhaled it was with a cloud of
steam. A thin layer of ice was forming over a half-drunk
pint on the adjacent table and Lupin's beard shimmered
with frost.

The stone came to rest on a letter. This time no one
spelled out loud. E. The counter moved on. A. Again it
moved. R. T.H. The spirits had spelled out *earth*.

I looked to Bella for a sign that she understood. She
looked just as confused as I felt, though her teeth were
chattering a little more.

The counter carried on its smooth journey over the
printed letters. This time it flowed over to F. Then I. Then
R. And finally E. *Fire*. Again the faces of my Ouija
companions were blank. The next word picked out by the

unseen forces, with excruciating slowness, was *Water*, then predictably, *Air*.

I grew angry. The spirit world is not a place I know much about. My dealings with it have been fleeting and unintended. In the 1890s I was tricked into wishing on an enchanted watering can and sentenced to eternity beyond the veil. Titus Brimtide, an arcane lawyer of standing, got me off on a technicality, but I served some time in the other dimension. It was like a desert souk, with people in white robes walking and talking under a white sun. There were great men there. I saw someone in the laurels of a roman emperor. I also saw Barry Torrington, who died trying to stage Whittleshin's first farmyard ballet. When one opened a door to this ream one never knew who or what would step through. It could be Marcus Aurelius. It could be Barry Torrington. It could be the tutu wearing cow that crushed him. Seemingly we had plucked out a cliche addled spirit who sought to impress us with mystic mumbo-jumbo. It would not have surprised me if next we were treated to the twelve signs of the zodiac.

Fortunately, we were spared a horoscope reading, instead the counter paused over the letters of a long sentence. *All Must Die And In The Centre Of The Triangle You U Find Out Y.*

Earth, fire, water, air. All must die, and in the centre of the triangle you will find out why.

Bella's spoke: "Oh spirits. We desire to know more. What else of the future can you tell us?"

The counter moved again, this time faster and with more violence, as if whatever we were questioning had better things to do and was growing tired of communicating with us. The table rocked as it jagged to each new letter. *The Biggest House Has The Biggest Secrets* it spelled out.

Bella asked if there was more but the stone stayed still. The cold faded from it until it had reached room temperature, and it continued to grow hotter. With cries of pain each of us drew our fingers away from the rock. The pub filled with the smell of singed Ouija board. Flames burst up from the centre of the circular stone until Lupin doused them with the half drunk beer. There was a fizz, a cloud of vapour and the smell of mulled ale.

"The biggest house," said Bella, looking at me. "In Wittleshin that's Pentdown Hall."

13

"Are you sure this is a good idea?" whispered Bella through her thick black balaclava.

I considered the question as I crept through the bushes towards Pentdown Hall. I could be betraying someone who had given me no concrete reason to doubt them, someone who employed me and who held the fate of my spirit tree in her hands. Equally we might be voluntarily entering the lair of a poison obsessed, baker slaughtering monster. It was a risky plan, but lives were at stake and we had had to find out what's going on.

"What she means is, do you feel comfortable breaking into your girlfriend's house?" said Lupin from my other side.

"She's not my girlfriend."

I heard Lupin giggle, "You'd like her to be, though. I haven't seen you this besotted since you gave that mesmerist all your savings."

"I wasn't besotted, and I didn't give them to her! She conned me!" I hissed back. Lupin was fond of bringing up my disastrous history with women. This was not the time nor the place for it.

"Fine," whispered Lupin. "But I knew as soon as we met her. You couldn't wait to get her out of bed and show her the fairy. You'd never have done that to Lionel Brimtide."

"I would if lives were at stake. And this is not about Lorna. I don't care about her at all."

"Good. Then you won't mind I ask her out then? Maybe I'll cook her a meal."

"Go ahead. Great idea, as we're already breaking into her house you might as well kill two birds with one stone. Leave her a note why don't you? 'Sorry about the burglary, can I take you on a date? Yours, A. Robber.'"

Lupin guffawed, another noise to add to the cacophonous racket he made crashing through the understory. "We could go on a double date. You could ask Felicity."

"Boys! No one is asking Lorna Brimtide out until we find out if she's a serial killer or not." whispered Bella. "And she wouldn't look at either of you anyway."

"What are you feeling so chirpy about, anyway?" I hissed to Lupin. "I thought you were scared of the dark."

"I'm scared of nothing," he replied loudly. It was a mistake to have brought Lupin when he was so close to Wolfdom. He was almost moon-mad. At this time of the month his cooking became more outlandish and his failures more spectacular. A few years earlier he has set fire to half the thatched roofs in Wittleshin while attempting to create edible fireworks. Gouts of molten chocolate and caramelised sugar had solidified on car windshields and Inspector Davies had threatened Lupin with a police caution.

"I shouldn't have invited you." I muttered.

"If you two are done bickering perhaps we could be serious for a moment? Are we actually going to do this? Because you know my reading of the Ouija board has been wrong in the past," said Bella.

"Yes," I said, with a decisiveness I did not feel. "We are doing this." I still hadn't worked out quite what my sentiments towards Lorna were, but whatever the workings of my heart my feelings for the village and its inhabitants were stronger. I could not bear to see Wittleshin marred by another murder. Lorna was a witch and she was an outsider. We had to suspect her.

"We could always just ask her what the secret in the big house is," said Lupin "That might work."

I shook my head. "If we ask her then we would reveal how much we know. She's bright, it took her ten minutes to figure out that I was a dryad. The less information she has the better."

"Fine, we won't ask her, but if she's up on Beech Ridge watching the Fae then why do we have to be so quiet about this. We could just walk straight up there."

"She might have familiars. Ravens or cats that could be her eyes and her ears. We can't be too careful," I said.

"Shhh," hissed Bella. "There's someone coming down the drive."

The three of us watched in silence as a chevron striped police car pulled up in front of the house. Inspector Davies got out, put on his mirrored aviator shades, hitched up his sagging trousers and walked over to pound on the door with the great leopard head knocker.

"What does he want?" whispered Lupin.

"He probably went down to my cottage to see if I went back there. Now he's here to ask Lorna if she's seen me," I replied. "I have the feeling he wants to section me."

We watched as Davies stood on the doorstep waiting for a reply. He scratched his behind with the comfortable pleasure of a man who has no idea he is being observed. The house remained quiet. No lights in the darkened windows. The policeman stared at the closed door for a few moments and then wandered back to his car to drive away.

"Looks like the coast is clear," said Lupin, standing up and crunching towards the house. He picked up a rock and tossed it in the air a few times, getting a feel for its weight. "I'll take out the window," he said.

"Wait! I know where she..." the crash of broken glass interrupted me as Lupin hurled the rock through the large windowpane. "...keeps the spare key," I finished, pointlessly. Lupin was already climbing through the hole he had created.

WE TIPTOED THROUGH THE HALLWAY. Apart from when we brought Mr Hipperty in the form of Esmy the fairy this was the first time I had been inside Pentdown Hall since Lorna had inherited the place.

From what I could tell she had not made many changes to her grandfather's decor. Austere portraits in oil paint still frowned down from the stairs. The sight of Sir Atticus Brimtide brought a knot to my stomach. Atticus had been the scourge of the garden. In the years of the old Prince Regent he had charged around on a huge black horse looking for idle workers to berate. His tirades would focus on the dire state of the lawn which was generally scarred with divots and hoofprints. Several times he had come close to striking me in arguments about manure. I would be wise to remember that this was the stock that had bred Lorna Brimtide.

The house was not deserted. From the large sitting-room to our left came the sound of deep, vibrating, tenor snores. I stuck my head through the doorway and saw Geoffrey. Empty bottles of Captain Brown's Strong Summer Ale surrounded the fairy.

"Where shall we start?" asked Bella, closing the door and cutting off the snores. I did not know what we were looking for. It could be a body, a vial of poison or a confession. There was every chance that we would not find the secret of the big house. For all I knew we had already walked past the metaphorical smoking gun with none of us noticing a thing. "We start in the Library!" I said, with the confidence of a general.

Not wanting to put on the bright overhead lights we lit the candles that stood on the ancient mahogany furniture. Lupin was becoming more reckless by the moment. Although he was still in the form of a chef his actions were becoming those of the beast he would soon be. He ran to the first of the shelves, giant structures that spanned the polished floorboards and the vaulted ceiling, and began pulling out books at random and throwing them to the floor.

"What are you doing!" I shouted.

"I'm looking for the secret," he replied, tossing aside another of Sir Lionel's esoteric tomes.

"You're not even checking what the books are!"

"I'll know the secret when I see it, and besides one of these books is probably a lever to open a secret passage. I know how these old houses work."

I scanned the shelves. For generations the Brimtides had been adding to their collection of esoteric tomes. It had reached its apogee under Lorna's grandfather, who had travelled to London to visit an antiquarian book sellers most weekends. In this room Lionel Brimtide had spent his life. He had occasionally walked the gardens and spoken to me of butterflies and roses, but away from the library he was a ghost. I had the company of his shadow alone, his substance was back in the Library with the book he had just read or the one that waited for him.

The shelves were without order. The Dewey System had no power here. Volumes on animal husbandry rubbed calf bound jackets with airport thrillers. Gargantuan encyclopaedias sat alongside slim pamphlets on the history of local churches. As I looked at the thousands of dusty spines I saw that Lupin's unique method of searching would be as profitable as any.

"Is there anything you can do to help?" I asked Bella, imploringly. "Something mystical?"

She thought for a moment, before smiling. "There might be something. I need you to find me a branch that splits into two forks, each one about this..." She held out her finger and thumb about an inch apart. "...thick. Go and do it now before my brother tears the house down."

I sprinted down the stairs and out into the night. I knew every inch of the grounds of Pentdown Hall, and my obsessive interest in how the plants were growing meant that I could head straight for a young hazel on the other side of the Italianate garden. I muttered a brief apology to the tree and reached for my secateurs, only to find them gone.

I felt naked, a horticulturist without secateurs was a knight without a sword. There was no time to ponder where they might be so I committed the gardener's ultimate crime; I ripped the branch away without using a sharp blade, leaving a jagged wound and tearing away a long heel of bark. The perfect site for infection to get in. It was poor husbandry, but we were living in desperate times. I promised myself that I would clean up the cut the next day and turned and ran back to the house.

BACK IN THE Library the pile of Lupin's discarded books was larger. He was wobbling at the top of a ladder that ran on brass rails around the shelves, heaving down books that opened their pages and fluttered as they fell. Sometimes I would glimpse complicated diagrams on the airborne pages. One caught my eye as it fell. In it strange lines ran from multi-coloured blobs into small paragraphs of dense text. I pulled the book through from the heap and flicked through it, eventually finding the pictogram and discovering that it displayed the political parties of 1920s Belize.

I passed the hazel stick to Bella, who declared it perfect and turned it around to hold the branch by its two forks.

It was clear she intended to use it as a dowsing rod. "I thought those things only worked for water," I said, as a blue paperback spun between us and knocked a vase from its plaster pedestal.

"They work best for water, but you can use them to find anything that gives out energy. Secrets give out energy, but it's very faint so I will need to concentrate hard." A huge book, bound in green leather and brass slammed into the floor beside her with a crash.

"Lupin!" Bella shouted. "Stop that right now. I need to focus."

The werechef sent down a companion volume. Bella strode to the bottom of the ladder and raised her foot. "If you don't stop right now then I swear to God I will kick down this ladder."

He paused, a book in hand, grinned and let it fall to the floor. Bella pulled the silver Boson's whistle from around her neck and gave a single ear piercing blast. "Lupin! Down!" she shouted.

Her brother woofed twice, then descended in silence.

We stood, hardly daring to breathe. Bella turned in a small circle in the middle of the Library, her attention on the end of her divining rod. Lupin stepped from the bottom of the ladder and tip-toed over to stand beside me, both of us fixated on the wobbling point of the stick.

The tip of Bella's tongue protruded from her mouth, her brow was furrowed. The whole room was focussed on that point of singularity, the quivering tip of the hazel stick, and then, suddenly, a loud beep sounded.

It broke the spell. Bella dropped the rod with a shout of anger. Lupin howled. I apologised and pulled my phone from my pocket to check the text message. It was from Lorna: '*Fairies on the move. Will follow them. L xx.*'

"Lorna says the fairies are moving out of camp. She will follow them," I told the others, leaving out the two kisses. "I'll turn my phone to silent. I'm sorry Bella, can we give it another go?"

Bella blew out her cheeks and picked the rod up. This time we kept quiet. The process was slow, over fifteen excruciating minutes Bella inched towards a shelf. The bottom half of the book rack was taken up by a series of large drawers, the top half stretched to the ceiling, My phone vibrated in my pocket.

'Still following. Looks like they are heading straight 4 Pent-down Hall!' No kisses this time and Lorna had written the message with enough haste to forgo proper English.

I dared not tell the others for fear of breaking the spell. We would surely be discovered. The rod was moving in slow motion. Finally it began to hover consistently over one drawer.

My nerve broke. "Right this one. Now run!" I shouted, ripping the drawer from its runners and sprinting out of the room with it under my arm.

14

W e hurried over the dark lawn. Shadows from the lime trees swelled towards us and bent away as lights moved between them down the drive. Faint bells, as if from a far-off village, followed the fairy procession. The Fae were bold tonight.

Under a layer of midsummer dew the garden was alive with speculation. The plants hummed with fear and false bravado. I'd heard such vegetable chatter before. It had proceeded the Night Gale of 1871 and the Great Storm of 1987. It was the sound of small things confronted by the impossibly large. Change was in the air.

We reached my cottage. I took a last look at the drive. It glowed like phosphorescent water. Swaying forms were moving beneath the limes. It was probably a trick of the shadows, but some of them seemed much larger than any fairy had the right to be. Fiddle music intermittently carried across the lawns. The playing didn't stop or start, just moved into and out of audible realms.

"Do you think I should call Lorna and get her to meet us here? I feel awful leaving her out there with the fairies, goodness only knows what they have planned." I said, bolting the door behind me, even as I spoke.

"We don't know if we can trust her." Bella's voice was stern. "And besides, how would you explain this?" She gestured to the mass of papers Lupin was spreading out on my kitchen table. The contents of the pilfered drawer. I conceded the point.

"We should have taken Geoffrey. It's him they're coming for," said Lupin.

"If we had him then the Fae would be coming here. Isn't that right Albertus?" said Bella.

I grunted and turned my attention to the odd mixture of maps, illustrations, pamphlets and loose sheets of paper that had filled the drawer. Publications from the Ordnance Survey nestled higgledy-piggledy with flyers for village fetes long past and posters for the 1986 Women's Institute summer party. When it came to litera-ture Sir Lionel had straddled the line between collector and hoarder. It was all irrelevant. Certainly, there was nothing that could be classed as the Ouija board's 'biggest secret.'

Lupin banged his head on the table in frustration. We were on the verge of giving up when I opened a plastic folder and a sheet that was much older than its neighbours fell out. It was folded into a yellowing square, and unlike the other bits and pieces it was not paper but animal hide. The surface was covered with ornate writing in what might have been brown ink and might have been dried blood.

"Look at this," I said. Lupin and Bella both stopped their search.

"What does it say?" asked Bella.

At first I struggled to read the antique script. It may have been an illusion caused by my lack of sleep, but the curls of the letters seemed to seethe and writhe before my eyes - maybe I just needed glasses. Eventually I adjusted to the text and began to read it aloud.

"And there shall be a place that sits on the confluence of three lines,"

"That's Wittleshin," interrupted Bella.

"And in that place there will come times when the longest day of the summer shall combine with the fullest night of the moon."

"That's tomorrow," added Lupin.

I gave them both a quieting glare and carried on reading aloud from the crumbling ancient text.

"And on those days should those who know may open a gateway to the invisible kingdom, and draw of the power there within." The words danced before my eyes, dissolving, mixing and recombining until they resolved into a legible paragraph.

"The key is made of four. Four sacrifices on four days. On the first of earth, on the second of fire, the third of water. On the night of the moon one of the air must be offered in the centre of the triangle. Thus will the power be released and the true wish granted."

I put down the vellum scroll. For a few moments none of us spoke. Eventually I got up and put the kettle on. If the situation called for anything it called for a cup of hot tea.

BELLA TOOK a sip from her mug and let out a sigh. "Okay. The first sacrifice has to be Geoffrey. But why would he be *One of Earth*?"

"That's easy," I replied. "He was a property developer. He bought and sold land. Personally, if I was carrying out the murders I would have chosen one of the farmers, or even a gardener, but I can see how Mr Hipperty could be considered of earth, just about.

"Right. Then Mr Fairchild the baker. He spent all his time working with ovens, so it's easy to see how he would be the *One of Fire*. Whoever is responsible has been following the script so far. Which means the murder they will commit tonight will be the *One of Water*," said Bella.

"Any sailors in the village?" asked Lupin.

"We are a hundred miles from the sea," snapped his sister.

"Fishermen?" he suggested.

"No one you could consider a professional, though I think there is an angling club that fishes on the river," I said.

"Seems unlikely. Come on, think." Bella again.

"Firemen. They use hoses," said Lupin. His sister and I shook our heads. There had not been a fire station in Wittleshin since the 1860s.

We rejected ice skaters, steam engineers, lock keepers and divers, both scuba and high. A few moments passed in silence. The conversation Bella had been dragged into the day before came back to me. Tea spurted from my mouth as I remembered Mrs Dobson's squeaking toilet. "What about Steve the Plumber? He works with water."

"I've got his number," Lupin growled. "From when he came round to fix the boiler, the swindling rip-off merchant charged us..."

Bella cut off her brother's rant by placing a hand over his. "Just phone him," she said.

I watched without breathing, hoping that Lupin would end the call with a 'hello' and a muttered apology for disturbing him so late, but the phone seemed to ring and ring. Eventually the werewolf shook his head and pressed the button to hang up. "No answer," he said.

"Maybe he's just gone to bed, it is late," suggested Bella.

"Not likely. Not with his emergency call out rate. I'd bet he sleeps with his telephone on his chest," said Lupin.

I said nothing, but I was inclined to agree with him. In all my many years I'd never met a plumber who didn't delight in the midnight callout and the good it could do his bank account. "He lives in one of the Mill Cottages, number three I think. Lupin why don't you go round there and see if you can rouse him."

The werewolf chef pushed back his chair hard enough to send it across the room. I winced as it clattered into the far wall. There was clearly wolf blood in his veins. Tomorrow morning Bella would have to carry out her monthly labour — tying him up in the beer cellar of the Bull and Firkin.

"Lupin," I called after him. "Be gentle."

"What do we do now?" asked Bella once her brother had loped into the night. By now Lupin was showing no fear of the dark. A howl sounded from beyond the herb garden.

"Go through the papers in the drawer again. There

might be something we have missed," I said, hoping for some time to think. I got out my map of Wittleshin and the surrounding parishes and made two marks on it. The first where Geoffrey Hipperty's body was found on the top of Beech Ridge, the second on the opposite side of the village where I had made the upsetting discovery of Mr Fairchild's corpse in the ditch. With a ruler and a marker pen I drew a thick black line between the two points. Bella stopped sorting through the papers and watched me.

"This is the base of our triangle," I said. "So the next murder will be here." I pointed to a point halfway along the line then drew my finger up at 90 degrees so it formed the third point of a triangle, hovering over a collection of old farm buildings. "Or Here." I did the same on the other side, my finger above a bend in the River Whittle.

"You're assuming it's an equilateral," said Bella.

"What?"

"You're assuming it's an equilateral triangle. That the sides are all the same length. It doesn't have to be. It could be a right angle triangle, or an isosceles. The next murder could be here." She pointed to a random point on the map. "Or here." She pointed to the Bull and Firkin. "Or anywhere, really."

I conceded the point. But in my experience mystic forces worked with the most prosaic geometry available. Who has ever heard of a protective oval or a satanic deca-hedron? When dealing with the spirit world moons were full or they were crescent shaped and the points of a pentangle were all as fat and malevolent as each other. I was about to explain this to Bella when we were inter-rupted by the ringing of my phone. I looked down at the screen, hoping that it was Lupin calling to say he had just roused an angry Steve the Plumber from his bed, but no, the screen read Lorna Brimtide. I crossed my fingers and pressed the button to answer.

"Albertus?" The voice on the other end of the line was tearful and ragged, she sounded distraught.

"Lorna what's wrong? What's happened?" My voice was flat and unconvincing.

"I've been burgled!"

"Oh goodness, no! That's terrible. Tell me what happened. The last thing I heard from you was that you were following the fairies towards Pentdown Hall. Do you think it could have been them?" Deception was not in my nature and I found evasion almost painful.

"I hate this village. I wish I'd never left London. If it wasn't for you and Bella and Lupin being so nice to me I'd pack my bags and leave right now."

I made a face. A pained wince, as if I were trying to squeeze all the guilt from my head. "Do you think it was the fairies?" I repeated.

"No, they did it before the fairies arrived," she spluttered. "It was one of you villagers. Some farmer or game-keeper. I thought murdering one another was enough to you people busy."

"Please Lorna. I promise we will solve the burglary later, but we have murders to worry about first. You were watching the fairies. Do you think they could have been up to something?"

"I don't think so. They just wanted their Esmy back. They all gathered around the house and started chanting something, then Geoffrey came to the front door as if he was in a trance. They sang to him and he walked off up the hill with them. It was only after they had gone that I found out I had been burgled. The window by the door was smashed and the Library completely turned over. It's horrible Albertus and I'm worried that it could be the murderer."

"Do you know what they've taken?" I asked. I sounded like stranger, callous and uncaring.

"No," Lorna sobbed. "I hadn't had time to go through the library yet. I had no idea what was there. How could I know what's not there now? It was all grandad's stuff!"

"So no valuables are missing? Computers, jewellery?" I asked.

"I don't think so, the only thing I can be sure is missing is one drawer from the library. There's just a space where it used to be."

Bella was trying to get my attention. Waving a piece of paper she had just found in my face.

"I don't feel safe up here on my own Albertus. Could I come down to your cottage?" said Lorna.

"Could you come down to my cottage?" I mused, looking at Bella.

She shook her head and slammed the piece of paper down on the table, stabbing at the headline with her index finger. It was a recipe: *'Perfect Elf Violet Cream Buns, Every Time!'*

"No," I said down the telephone. "I'm not in my cottage. I'm nowhere near the cottage. I'm out hunting for the killer. Sorry Lorna." I hung up.

"Do you think she did it?" asked Bella.

"Maybe." I replied.

There was a noise from outside. The door swung open and Lorna stood framed in the rectangle of dark.

Her eyes flicked from me to Bella and down to the distinctive drawer and the papers that lay scattered between us.

She turned without speaking and disappeared into the night.

15

On the map the buildings had been regular little squares, a complement they had not earned. Their outlines were slumped against the night sky with not a straight line or even surface among them. Even the ground they stood on felt warped and close to collapse.

I gave the door to the main barn a shove and it swung open with a long creak. My eyes had adjusted to the starlight but they struggled with the gloom inside. In places the roofing had come away from the rafters and the moon shone on rusted machinery and empty feed sacks. I stepped in and rats scuttled away to watch me from the darkest corners. The light of my flashlight was enough to chase them off, but it ruined my night vision and drew the dark peripheries of the barn about my head. I opened my mind, hoping to hear the welcome chatter of plants, little green friends that I could enlist in my detective quest, but was disappointed. The place was a wasteland.

Swinging the beam of the torch I caught empty bottles and tins of chemicals. Their labels had moulded away. The corroded metal cylinders oozed and several of the bottles had smashed. My throat burned and my eyes stung. This was the herbicide store of some long bankrupt farmer. I had wandered into a trove of defunct weedkillers that had probably been banned for causing cancers or the sudden death of newts. To a dryad they were deadly.

I knocked over an empty container and my heart thumped. I wished that I had someone with me for this macabre treasure hunt, but it had seemed sensible to send both Bella and Lupin down to the River Whittle, the other hypothetical point of the equilateral triangle. If the body had ended up in the water then there was a far greater area for them to search. They would have to peer into black millponds and creep under curtains of willow. Who knew where the corpse could have floated to or snagged?

Of course we had no idea if anyone had been killed at all. Lupin had come back to the cottage to report that there was no answer from Steve the Plumber's cottage, and that his van was not in the driveway, but for all we knew he could be away visiting relatives.

The rotting hulk of a combine harvester blocked my path and I picked my way around the rusting spikes of its blade. On the other side of the harvester lay a mouldering heap of grain, harvested some summer past and left there to rot, food only for fungus and rodents. I skirted it and carried on towards the back of the building, praying that my feet encountered nothing deadly on the way.

Was this the crime scene a city witch would choose? I
didn't think so, but then, for someone following the
ancient parchment there wouldn't be much choice over
venues. I tossed my head and groaned but my shame was
too rooted to shake loose. If Lorna was innocent our
actions were unforgivable. She had moved to a new
village, under what turned out to be troubling circumstances, and believed that she was making connections in
the local community, only to discover the people she
thought of as friends had lied and set her up. They had
invaded her sanctuary and burgled her. Witches might be
crafty creatures but they had feelings, and we had hurt
them. If Lorna had not wanted to harm to the people of
Whittleshin before tonight she almost certainly did now.

I worried for the safety of my home tree. Among the
many wickednesses attributed to witches was a love of
vengeance. Here in the Whit Valley a tale was told from
centuries before I was born. The inhabitants of a village
found a witch draining the milk from their cattle. They
drove her away with stones. The witch was grievously
injured and it was thought that she would die in the
woods. But the witch did not die. She climbed a tree and
cast a spell on the village. They were possessed by a love
of the stones they had thrown. Men knocked down their
wooden houses and replaced them with stone. Granite
dust filled the air, chisels became the wedding present for
a bride and hammers for a newborn. Work began on a
stone cathedral. And when those who had begun it had
died, and their children died, and their children's children had died, and the village had become a small and
prosperous city, the cathedral was finally finished. The
people gathered under the stone spire and all were killed

when it fell upon them. Only then did the witch climb from her tree to sit on the rubble. It was a magnificently ludicrous tale of revenge, but these pearls of exaggeration often form around a grain of truth.

Such were my concerns as I reached the damp and disintegrating back wall of the barn. I tried to pull myself together. I was as yet unharmed by herbicides or axes and I had found no dead bodies. Cadavers had been crossing my path too often of late. I wanted to report the area clear and get home to my bed, it felt like I hadn't slept in days. Edging past the rotting grain and the disintegrating farm-yard machinery I headed towards the open door. It was visible as a faint coral pink rectangle. This was the day of the summer solstice, the shortest night of the year, and the sun had snuck up on me. Dawn broke over the ancient chalk hills.

I left the barn and turned back to Wittleshin, which lay in the still-dark valley below. After a few steps I sunk deep into a muddy puddle. Water topped my boot, soaking my woollen sock, and shocking me into dropping my flashlight. Just my luck to end up in a puddle when we'd had no rain for weeks and the ground was dry and cracking. I bent down and rummaged in the dirty water until I found my now useless light, before squelching away. Had I been less tired the incongruity of the situation would have hit me earlier, but in my sleep-deprived state I was halfway home before I turned and ran back up the hill.

I found the telltale puddle and followed the small trickle of water that ran away from the barn and into the gloom of the surrounding woods. Ahead of me was a low single story building, even more decrepit than the barn. There was a white van parked next to it.

I knew what would be on the van before I reached it, and sure enough there it was, sign-written in bright blocky letters: *Steve's Plumbing Services, Ltd.* I checked the front seats and found them empty, and so steeling myself, I prepared to enter the derelict building.

My wet flashlight was now as useless and it was hard to see anything inside. The building had once been a chicken coop. Feathers coated every surface and the walls were lined with shelf like roosts, all of them long deserted. My eyes began to adjust to the dark and I made out a few more features. A huge stack of feed sacks, some of them empty, some of them still half-full, took up most of the floor. Above the sacks ran a pipe, presumably part of a system that had once fed the drinking troughs. It was streaming water.

Running my hand along the pipe I felt a series of scratches. In the gloom it was hard to see, but under my fingers they felt a like they might be runic symbols carved into the soft lead with the tip of a nail. A gash in the metal was the source of the waterfall, its sides gleamed, freshly exposed and as yet unoxidised. This was not the effect of age and everyday corrosion - the plumbing had been sabotaged.

I crouched down low enough for the splashes to wet my face and scanned the area under the ruined pipe. A shape among the feed sacks. Steve the Plumber lay on his back, his dead eyes looking up at the ceiling. He had answered his final call-out.

16

I woke with my head swimming in the confused residue of deep sleep. I had dreamed of Lorna. Me and Steve the Plumber had driven her from the Bull and Firkin where she had been downing pints of milk at the bar. We'd reached Pentdown Hall to see Lupin driving my ride-on lawn mower over the herbaceous borders and Steve had danced off to fix a leak in the marmalade tank.

"This is not a normal morning," my brain tried to tell me, "something has happened." The first odd thing I noticed was the noise. There was nothing from the willow warblers, sparrows and chiff-chaffs that lived in the hedges of the herb garden. Instead I could hear the steady droning call of crickets and grasshoppers. I sat upright. The chirping of the insects meant that the grass in the borders and the wild-flower meadows was hot. The dawn chorus was over, the sun high in the sky, the day well advanced. I had meant to rest my eyes for a moment but my exhausted mind had shut down.

I shot out of bed, propelled by adrenaline and memories of the night before. One cup of tea, I told myself, just one cup of tea in the garden, pretending this was a carefree summer's day, then I would put my sleuth hat back and try to stop anyone else getting murdered in Wittleshin.

I took my mug and drank it on the stone bench outside my cottage. The stored energy of the sun radiated from the seat below me and the wall behind me, soothing away the cold, abandoned farm buildings I had visited the night before. It is no doubt unhealthy to depend on one thing for refuge, recreation and employment, but the garden at Pentdown Hall was all I had ever known. In a real sense I was nothing without it.

A bumble-bee dipped between flowers of lychnis and achillea. The warm air was scented with thyme. I drank in the smells, sights and sounds of the garden, drained the tea and strode back into the cottage. I failed before, but now I had a life to save.

The phone rang for a minute before there was an answer.

"Hello?" Bella's voice was thick with sleep and I guessed that I had woken her. Not surprising, she'd had as little rest as I had over the past few days, and would have had to coax her almost werewolf brother down into the cellar after they had returned from the river.

"Bertie? Is that you? What time is it?"

"It's almost one," I said.

Bella responded with crude words and there were a series of crashing thumps as she ran around her chaotic bedroom getting dressed. I had told Bella and Lupin about Steve the Plumber's end the night before, and we had all agreed that there was nothing we could do in our fatigue. Bella and I had concluded that it would be best to get some sleep and then reconvene the next day. Neither of us expected it to be this late.

"Okay. I'm good. What's the plan?" she said, breathlessly.

"Right," I said. "This time we have the advantage. If what the parchment says is true then we know precisely where the next victim will be." I had marked Steve the Plumber's body on the map before I fell asleep and connected it to the other two deaths with thick lines. The centre of the triangle was Wittleshin Village Hall.

"Okay, so how do we stop it?" asked Bella.

"We start by identifying the victim. We know they will be someone of air. Though I can't work out who that could be. We don't have any pilots in the village and there hasn't been a windmill here for a hundred and fifty years."

Bella was quiet for a moment. "I know," she said, suddenly. "Old Mrs Dobson and the ladies from the Women's Institute. What do I always say about them? That they are gas bags, full of hot air. You can't get closer to an air-person than a walking, talking wind bag! The seeker from the parchment is going to kill one of those poor old dears in the Village Hall!"

"Those posters Mrs Dobson gave you to put up for the Women's Institute summer party, what do they say?" There was a brief noise as Bella sorted through the piles of mystic rubbish that covered every surface in her room.

"I've found it! There is a big picture of a cake and below it says: please come and join us for our midsummer party, Wittleshin Village Hall, 12.30p.m."

"So it's started already? We might be too late!"

Hurrying out of my cottage and up past Pentdown Hall I allowed myself a quick glance at the rose and wisteria covered frontage and noticed that someone had boarded up the window we had smashed the night before but there was no movement behind the windows. If Lorna was the killer I wondered what her motive was, what would she ask from the invisible kingdom? Would it be riches? An other worldly hoard of treasure that would ensure she never again had to make a lavender scented candle? I will never understand those who kill, those who kill for money least of all.

So ran my thoughts as I turned onto the lane and headed down towards the centre of the village. Bella had arranged to wait outside the village hall. I hoped that inspiration would strike me on the walk, because at that moment I didn't have a clue what we would do when we met. As ever, I kept my eyes downcast, wary of my Gardener's Walk, but a bowed head would not deter Felicity Jenkins. Once more I could not pass her house without being spotted. Normally I would curse under my breath, but today I unleashed a loud string of oaths into the warm summer air.

"Oooh, Albertus, have I caught you at a bad time? Are you late for something?" Felicity was wearing an apron and was carrying a carpenter's metal ruler.

I fought an internal battle, one that only lasted a fraction of a second but still tested every moral fibre of my being. My good nature won out. As a gardener, a tree and an Englishman I was unable to tell her to get lost. I slowed down, politely.

"Sorry Felicity. I've been a little stressed recently."

"That does surprise me Albertus. I always thought horticulture was so soothing. Very good for the mental health, I hear. Is it those two bodies you found?"

Three, I thought to myself, but I didn't bother to correct her.

"Well you shouldn't worry about it, just rotten luck that's all, nothing to get worked up about. You should focus on your job. Such a lovely relaxing life, just pottering around with plants all day in the sun."

"It has its moments," I muttered through gritted teeth.

"Oh, is that new lady up there giving you a hard time?" said Felicity, sounding thrilled. "I told you she looked full of herself, I could tell from the very first moment I saw her. Not our type at all. A Londoner. You know I saw her earlier today walking down the hill carrying a huge tray of cakes. I felt like telling her to keep her hands off our lovely things. She's obviously going to enter the Women's Institute cake baking competition, as if there weren't enough tarts in that building already."

I stopped walking.

Felicity kept blabbering. "She's probably baked some city style cake, gluten-free or whatever, but let me tell you, Albertus, it won't be any match for my grandmother's rock cakes. I've measured every single one of them, they are perfect!" She waved the ruler around. "I ought to throw a rock cake at your fancy Londoner! Would that cheer you up Albertus? Would it make you feel better?" Felicity beamed at me.

It was sweet of her to offer to assault my boss, but I

had no time to process the compliment. "What time is the judging?" I gabbled, sounding desperate for baked goods.

"It starts in twenty-five minutes. I'm just about to take my entry down to the hall. I always try to leave it to the last minute, to conserve the freshness, it makes all the difference. Particularly when sultanas are involved." Felicity winked, as if this were to mean something to me.

I nodded. "We have to get down there now. We need to stop anyone eating Lorna's cakes."

"Oh, well I'm sure they are not that bad," said Felicity, happily. "But you're right, maybe we should give them a miss. Hang on one moment, I'll collect my bake and we can go together."

Felicity disappeared inside her cottage and came out carrying a metal tray covered by a gingham cloth. I could see that there were a series of bumps underneath the chequered material.

"How many cakes are you allowed to enter?" I asked.

"Well this year we are doing something different," explained Felicity, excitedly. "It's a miniature round. We saw it on the television. Everyone enters six small cakes. They can be cupcakes or brownies, or even miniature sponges, anything really, but each one has to be identical. It's very exciting, a whole new thing for us, as soon as I saw it I thought to myself 'that's just the thing to help bring the image of the Women's Institute into the modern era.' I didn't know if old Mrs Dobson would go for it, she's used to winning every year with that Victoria sponge she's been baking since 1953, but in the end I managed to talk her round."

I nodded along as we walked down the hill. The parchment had said one of air would be killed next, but only one, which led me to suspect that only one of the six cakes the poisoner had entered would be laced with elf violet. If I didn't identify the murderous treat the ladies of the Women's Institute were in for a deadly game of dessert roulette.

"Would you like me to carry that tray for you?" I asked, remembering my manners. Felicity Jenkins froze in her tracks, the habitual smile wiped from her bright red lips. She looked very serious. "Albertus, you know that I feel very warmly towards you. I think that you are a wonderful person, and one that I would sincerely like to get to know better. But no one gets to touch my cakes before the W.I. judging. It's just far too important an occasion."

"Okay," I said, chastened.

"I am sorry Albertus. I'm not saying that you would cheat, or that you might be in league with any of the other combatants, but what if you were to look under the cloth? Then the whole process of anonymous judging would have been ruined. I would have been compromised."

"What do you mean the process of anonymous judging?"

"Well no one can know whose cake they are tasting. That way lies corruption. Vote buying, intimidation! Favouritism would be rife. It would change from a baking competition into a worthless popularity contest. No one must know who baked which cake."

17

As we agreed Bella was waiting outside the village hall. The little Victorian building was decked out in its midsummer finery. The lintels and door were freshly painted in a glossy red that clashed wonderfully with the yellow pompom marigolds in the window boxes. A large canvas sign promising '*cakes and jam today!*' hung from the white picket fence. From the flag pole fluttered a large union jack, reserved for fetes and royal weddings. Hanging baskets of trailing petunias and lobelias dripped wetly onto the hot pavement, evidence of their recent watering. The Women's Institute would not let the spectre of a wilting leaf ruin their special day. In front of all the pomp of an English summer tea-party Bella, the worried looking goth, looked incongruous and uninvited.

I said goodbye as politely as I could to Felicity, who wore the stern expression of a soldier about to enter a war zone. There was a determined firmness to her jaw that I had never seen in her before and she neglected to give Bella the jealous stare reserved for my female friends. The blond divorcee carried the tray of cakes as if she were an acolyte bearing an offering to her ancient god.

"Good luck!" called Bella, her tone bordering on sarcastic.

I hushed her and told her about our problem; that Lorna was inside and had entered the baking competition. I think I might have come across as breathy and panicked, because Bella tried to reassure me. "Calm down, Bertie. First, we don't really know if Lorna is trying to poison anybody. Second, the solution is easy. We just stop anyone from eating her entry, sneeze on it, knock it on to the floor, spill a cup of coffee on it. Simple."

"The entries are anonymous, Bella. We won't have any idea which one is Lorna's."

The revelation only threw her for a second. "What was the recipe we found? Perfect elf violet cream buns every time? We just find the cream buns and get rid of those." Bella seemed pleased with her plan. I wished I had her confidence.

"Okay, but if there is any confusion I'm going to stop the whole party. I'll set off the fire alarm."

"Right, let's do this," said Bella, and together we turned and entered Wittleshin village hall.

OUR FIRST IMPRESSION was of bunting. It hung in multi-coloured strips from every surface and beam an old lady on a step ladder could reach. Some flags sported tiny union jacks, others polka-dots and stripes, and yet more displayed the bright primary shades of the fairground. The strings hung in such effusive disarray that it felt like the village hall was the lair of some giant patchwork spider.

Beneath the bunting-strewn ceiling stood small groups of chatting people. Most of them were old ladies of two distinct varieties; the first wore tea-cosy hats and bulky winter coats in varying shades of pastel. These pensioners hovered near the buffet and looked guilty about the tuna and cucumber sandwiches they had hidden in their handbags. The second group wore pearls and superior attitudes, they had most likely all submitted marmalade to the jam competition.

Both groups cast frequent possessive looks at the line of trestle tables that ran down the centre of the room. The better actors among them feigned an interest in the plant sale, or half-heartedly spun the tombola, but it was clear these were mere diversions, designed to convince the observer that no fig was given about the table and its contents.

The table itself was daunting both in its size and uniformity. I spotted what could have been Felicity's entry to the baking competition, a circular metal platter supporting a gingham cloth with six cake-shaped bumps underneath it. Next to it was another, identical in all regards except for the shape of the bumps. Next to that another, and opposite more. The table was laden with identical looking submissions, regulation cloths on regulation trays. There would be no undue favouritism in this bun-fight.

Bella and I looked at each other and she drew her finger across her neck.

I nodded my agreement and started scanning the walls for the fire alarm. It was very much time for Plan B. My visual quest was brought to an abrupt close as a heavy hand fell on my shoulder.

"Mr Oak," whispered the grating voice of Inspector Davies. From the smell of his breath he had already been at the tuna sandwiches. "How are you feeling today?"

"Fine Inspector, absolutely sane." I said, aware that my blithe answer was not backed up by my sweaty demeanour and nervously shifting pupils.

"I was hoping you would be here. I have something that I think might belong to you." He rummaged in the pocket of his coat and pulled out my battered but sharp secateurs, still sitting in their monogrammed leather holster. Our reunion felt like the first good thing to happen in an age, a glimmer of light through the streaming clouds.

"Thank you Inspector! Where were they?"

"Well that's the funny thing, Mr Oak. We found them in the middle of a crime scene," he said.

I was elated. If the police were treating the deaths as crimes then maybe I could hand this whole sorry mess over to them, the people who should have been investigating this whole thing from the very beginning.

Inspector Davies shattered my flimsy bubble of hope with his next words, spoken with an indecent relish. "We found them in the Library of one Miss Lorna Brimtide following a forced entry and burglary at her property. A crime that has left her most distressed indeed. Do you have any idea how they might have ended up there, Mr Oak?"

They say that lying is like exercising, the more you

work at it the better you get. I was proving the aphorism wrong. "Ummm..." I stammered. "...no?"

Inspector Davies stared at me for a long time. "Mr Oak, I am watching you. If I see you take even half a step out of line I'm taking you in to the station. Do you understand?"

"Yes," I said.

The corpulent policeman donned his mirrored shades and moved a few steps away to take up his position by the tuna sandwiches.

I could feel his eyes boring into the side of my head, and I fancied that I could hear the crunch of cucumber from between his jaws. I would have to tread carefully. It would be hard to stop anyone from getting poisoned from the back of a police van.

My search for the fire alarm continued in what I hoped was a covert manner. Rather than the little red box I hoped that they would encounter my eyes fell on the frosty stare of Lorna Brimtide.

If she was upset with me it did not show on her face. It was as if she had not even seen me. If she were she planning to murder someone within the next few minutes I would never have been able to tell, her eyes betrayed nothing. There was an iciness to her expression that could either come from not wanting to give away any emotion to a man who had hurt her, or from being a cold-blooded, multiple murdering, demon worshipping psychopath who should be stoned forthwith. I swallowed, steeled my nerve and started to walk towards her.

I had barely taken three steps before a hellish wailing shriek interrupted us. I ducked my head, convinced that our murderer had already opened the gates to the invisible kingdom, before realising that the ear-piercing scream was just feedback from the P.A. system, the prelude to announcements in village halls countrywide.

"Hello. Testing. Hello. Is this thing on?" came a faltering and elderly voice. At the end of the hall Mrs Dobson was fiddling with the bottom of a microphone.

"Can you hear me?" she asked, her voice blasting from the speakers loud enough to deafen the dead.

"Turn it down!" shouted Inspector Davies with his mouth full. I was glad I had moved out of tuna-spittle range. There was a series of amplified bumps and hisses, a few breaths, and then the voice of Mrs Dobson returned, this time at a more manageable volume.

"Is that better?" she asked.

"Yes dear," chorused the old ladies.

"Good, well thank you all for coming. First, I have an announcement from Inspector Davies. Could whoever owns the red Vauxhall Astra please move it? You're blocking the emergency exit." Heads twisted on wrinkled necks as the spectacled eyes of the audience searched for the guilty party. A tutting spread through the room as one of the ladies sidled out, car keys in hand. The Women's Institute summer party had claimed its first victim.

"Now," continued Mrs Dobson. "I'm pleased to announce that the winner of the flower arranging contest is..." she paused, building the tension like a practised show woman. "...Mrs Treedle."

Polite applause and resentful murmurs were directed towards Mrs Treedle, who punched the air and gurned.

"So it's on to the moment you have all been waiting for. The judging of the baking competition!"

Tense cheers from the crowd.

"As you know we have decided to try something different this year. Everyone who has entered the competition has baked six identical mini-cakes, treats or pastries. These will be judged on taste, texture, skill and uniformity in complete anonymity by a panel of expert judges."

She stopped and looked at a crumpled note in her hand. Clearly what she had to say next was complicated. "Bear with me dears. Righty-oh. Here's how the judging will work. There will be six judges. Each will award marks from one to ten, with decimal points allowed. The highest score and the lowest scores will be eliminated in the interest of fairness and the remaining scores added together to find the submission's final mark."

There was a hubbub of chatter as the waiting old ladies digested the regulations. I had never heard Mrs Dobson so coherent and precise.

"I will be the first judge," she continued. Outraged shouting followed this announcement. "Ladies, ladies please! Remember, if I give myself an artificially high mark, it will be discarded." This somewhat mollified the horde of amateur bakers, but a disgruntled undercurrent buzzed around the room.

"Lorna Brimtide has agreed to be the second judge - many of you will remember her grandfather, Sir Lionel Brimtide, who for many years opened our summer party, and I'm glad that, through Lorna, this esteemed family is continuing its ongoing association with the Women's Institute."

Those who did not know Lorna had entered the competition herself clapped nicely. Felicity Jenkins and the other who knew that she was competition booed discreetly. Would the murderer sail so close to the wind? Would she willingly put herself in the orbit of the poisoned bun? Officiating in the contest spoke of innocence or astonishing audacity.

"Inspector Davies has also agreed to judge." The applause this time was more fulsome. "And our vicar, Reverend Lucy." The vicar stood up with a relaxed smile and walked towards the low stage. She was in her element with old ladies and cake.

"Which means we still need two judges, ideally someone who has not entered the competition."

Bella raised her hand and shouted "Albertus, Albertus Oak!"

"Yes, that nice gardener, Albertus Oak," called one of the ladies.

"Yes! Albertus!"

I reminded myself to thank my friend for volunteering me for the deadly game of cake roulette, if I survived the process that was. Grinning through clenched teeth I made my way up to the circular table on the stage.

"Which just leaves us needing one more judge. Are there any volunteers?"

I hoped that Bella would be as quick to put herself forward as she was me, but before she opened her mouth once more Felicity was barrelling towards the stage clamouring for her own inclusion. Mrs Dobson was in no position to resist such a forceful application, and so there we were: The Wittleshin Six.

18

We half-dozen valiant judges took our places around a small table, covered with a table-cloth so white and well-starched that it could only have come from Mrs Dobson's personal collection.

Lorna sat opposite me, with Inspector Davies to her left. The policeman still wore his ludicrous sunglasses. I wished Lorna had them on instead. Her eyes flashed, either with anger, hurt or murderous intent. Reverend Lucy, seated to my right, did not seem to have noticed any atmosphere, and kept up a stream of good-natured pleas-antries of the sort that served her well outside the church gates every Sunday.

I was sweating and I could feel the entirety of Inspector Davies' bristling presence focussed on me. My movements were false and stiff as I tried to avoid making any twitches or gestures that could be construed as madness or criminal intent. The cause was not helped by Felicity Jenkins who was seated to my left. She had placed her hand high on my thigh and showed intentions of sliding it higher still.

I wondered if I could explain our danger before Inspector Davies dragged me from the room. Judging from the way he fingered his handcuffs I guessed I would only have about five words to do it in, not enough to warn the other judges of the mortal threat we faced.

I tried to smile at the vicar, whose mouth was moving up and down in a manner that suggested she might be talking to me, but all I could hear was the pounding of blood in my ears. In the crowd of expectant faces I searched for Bella's dark-rimmed eyes, but found only the wrinkled and expectant brows of the elderly ladies. I was on my own.

"And may the best baker win!" called Mrs Dobson.

The first tray of cakes was laid in front of us with some ceremony. The Reverend was the first to act, reaching forward to pull away the gingham cloth and reveal six small angel cakes. To me they looked identical, but I am a better judge of gardens than I am baked goods.

Felicity reached into her handbag and pulled out her metal ruler. "Ah-ha, just as I thought, there is a difference of at least 1.5 centimetres in the rise."

I wondered if she always carried the precision measuring equipment around with her, or if she had somehow suspected that she might end up on the judging panel. I realised that she could well be my chief ally in spotting the poisoned cake. If Lorna had slipped in a toxic pastry, then she would need to have included some sort of clue, something that would tell her which one she ought to avoid eating. If anyone were to spot this irregularity it would be Felicity Jenkins.

"Quite," remarked old Mrs Dobson. "I blame a cheap electric oven with improper heat dispersal. Probably made by china-men."

"Oh I don't know, they look delicious to me," said the Reverend, allowing her natural goodness to come through, though we all knew there was no place for that kind of thing in a cake baking competition.

Inspector Davies' had reached out faster than I had ever seen him move, and his cheeks were already bulging with cake, the crumbs cascading down his chin like rocks in a patisserie avalanche.

Lorna was avoiding my eyes, prodding at her cake with one manicured finger. She reached down, picked it up and took a bite. I said a prayer to the god of oak trees and bit into my piece.

Soft, crumbly, a light texture without being too dry, and no throat-squeezing, heart-stopping cardiac failure, just the way I liked my cakes. I resolved to score high. No sooner than I had written my mark (8.4, a strong start but with room for exceptional cakes later on) than the next of the gingham trays was winging its way towards the table. The cloth was whipped away to reveal a tray of fragrant and glistening apple Danishes. Never had a missile of death looked so tasty.

Six hands reached out. I tried to put into practice the things that Geoffrey Hipperty had said made him Harrogate Poker Champion two times over and studied Lorna for potential tells. Had she hesitated before picking up her pastry? Or moved to grab one that by rights should not have belonged to her? Did I detect a twitch in her delicate cheek? I thought not.

Too late I realised that although I had been following

the first part of Geoffrey's advice, to search your oppo-
nents face for telltale signs, I was ignoring the second
part - I was not keeping my emotions and suspicions
secret at all. I was certain that my face was pale, it felt like
all the blood had drained from my body. I was sweating,
and my gaze lurched from Lorna to the others around the
table as I tried to look for the early signs of elf violet
poisoning.

"Are you all right dear? You look just like my Wilfred
before he had his third stroke." asked Mrs Dobson from
across the table.

"Yes."

The Reverend placed a comforting hand over mine.
"Are you sure Albertus? You don't look very well at all to
me. You're not diabetic are you? I only ask because
diabetes is God's way of saying 'don't eat all that cake!'"

"You look disturbed Mr Oak, almost deranged. You're
not going to do anything you might regret, are you?" said
Inspector Davies, and he made a small movement that
might have been an adjustment to his belt and might
have been a subtle reminder that he had his handcuffs at
the ready.

"I'm fine. I just... I mean I have..." I searched for
answers, "...I have gluten intolerance. I'm allergic to
cake!"

Lorna shot me a withering look. "Then why did you
volunteer to judge a baking contest? Go home, let
someone else judge." It was the first time she had spoken
to me since catching me red-handed with her stolen
possessions. I don't know why I should have expected
kinder words, but I did.

"Yes dear, it was very kind of you to volunteer to

judge, but you really didn't have to, not with your condition. Why don't you have a nice cup of tea and let someone else take over," said Mrs Dobson.

There was no way I could let someone else take over. To do so would have exposed one of the old ladies to the danger I was in. There was no way I could let them eat cake; I would never forgive myself.

"No, no," I protested. "It's a very mild intolerance. More of a dislike if I'm honest. Most of its psychological. I'll be fine."

Lorna would not let me get away with it. "Okay Albertus, my question still stands, even if the terms are different. If you don't like cake then why are you judging a cake eating contest?" She was skewering me with all the ruthlessness of a serial poisoner.

"Well," I said, feeling the five pairs of eyes around the table boring into me, as well as the confused stares of everyone in the room who was not privy to the life-or-death conversation taking place on the stage. "If everyone on the judging panel liked cake then it would hardly be fair would it? Everyone would mark highly just based on the fact that it was cake they were eating. No, far better to have a member of the jury who has to fight down each mouthful, that way each of my points has been truly earned."

The other members looked at me quizzically. An unbroken ring of scepticism that only faltered when Inspector Davies could not hold out any longer and stuffed one of the apple Danishes into his cavernous mouth.

The next hour passed in a blur of cake crumbs and conversation. We tasted petit fours, Swiss rolls, sponges of all hues and textures, fruit cakes, rum cakes and plum cakes, whoopee pies and tea cakes. The vicar, Mrs Dobson and Felicity had resorted to the old wine taster's trick of sampling the tiniest morsel and leaving aside the rest. After each bite they took a sip of milky tea to cleanse their palates. It would not save them. Elf violet was fatal in the most tiny doses.

I was saving my tea, planning to spill it over the tray once I had identified which one might hold the poisoned cake. It would not be the first time a nice cup of tea had saved a life. Lorna was eating most of the submissions set in front of her, except for a particularly literal rock-cake. Inspector Davies stuffed each baked fancy into his capacious maw like a man who thought he might never get the chance to eat again, and how right he may have been. I had given up on the ostentatious displays of distaste that accompanied my earlier rounds and adopted a look that I hope spoke of resigned stoicism.

My routine for each round of tasting was almost identical. My heart rate began to rise as soon as I spotted the gingham platter borne towards our table. To a soundtrack of blood pumping in my temples I would scan the faces around the table, hoping one of them might recognise the bumps under the cloths as their creation. Next, as the cloth was removed, I studied judges' expressions, particularly Lorna's, hoping to see the face of a murderer reunited with their weapon of choice, whatever that might look like. I then turned my attention to Felicity and her precision measuring equipment, hoping that she would identify the toxic confection in that manner. Next I watched to see if anyone reached for the wrong cake, or hesitated in taking a bite. Finally, I checked for signs of fatal convulsions in both myself and my companions.

In this manner the afternoon was nibbled, swallowed and sipped away. The trestle table emptied as the crowds of old ladies slipped into corners to gossip about what had been on the television the night before.

A tiny flame of hope kindled in the damp wood of my heart. There were only three platters left and no-one had died yet. Perhaps, despite my worries, there would be no murder.

The last tray but two was set down and the atmosphere around the table seemed to change. The gingham cloth was removed and what I saw hit me like a punch in the guts. On the tray before me stood six plumply oozing cream buns.

19

Six identical cream buns, soon to be eaten. Six living judges, soon to be five. Time slowed as I reached for my mug of now cold tea. Surely no one would care to eat their treat after the platter had been doused in a tepid infusion of breakfast blend. At the same time Felicity leant forward with her ruler, searching for the inconsistencies that could spell the difference between a 7.8 and an 8.3. Her head was inches from the table as she supported her weight on her arms, craning her neck to gaze at the bun from its own level. In an attempt to peer closer still she crabbed sideways and caught my mug with her elbow. Tea fell into my lap in beige cascade. I jumped up as the liquid hit me. There was a great commotion around the table, handkerchiefs were offered to me from all directions but that of Inspector Davies. Felicity sought to take things into her own hands and dab me down herself. "I'm fine. I'm fine!" I said and sat down.

Something changed in the confusion. The buns looked more or less the same, but the angle I was seeing them from had altered. Someone had used the pandemonium of the spillage to change the position of the buns, either by swapping one or spinning the tray. Tea dripped down the inside of my trousers and the blood drained from my face.

"Come on Albertus. It was only a bit of a spill, but you look as though someone just died. Your favourite trousers were they?" ribbed Inspector Davies.

I didn't reply, but watched in silent horror as five hands reached out to pick up cream-buns and five mouths opened in sweet-toothed anticipation. It was now or never.

"STOP!!"

The doors of the village hall burst open. A deep northern voice called out once more. "STOP RIGHT NOW! THE BLOODY BUNS ARE BLOODY-WELL POISONED!" All turned to the cause of the interruption. There stood Geoffrey the Fairy, tiny hands on girlish hips, our silver-haired saviour.

Inspector Davies threw his bun back onto the tray uneaten. "Bleeding gypsies!" He roared. Knocking over his chair and thundering off the stage. "I'll give you what for! I'll send you all back where you came from!" He carved a bad tempered path through the old ladies towards the tiny childlike figure, who turned and fled with him in close pursuit.

"Oh dear," said the Reverend. "He does seem rather angry, doesn't he?"

"Yes dear, but gypsies are as gypsies do," said Mrs

Dobson. "Let's get on with the competition." She raised her bun once more. The others did the same. With Inspector Davies gone it was my chance to act. I sprung from my chair and slapped what I was now certain was the poisoned cream bun away from the mouth of its intended victim.

20

All eyes watched the cream bun trace an elegant parabola through the air, spinning gently end over end, shedding globs of cream like a disintegrating satellite. It hit the wall with a fat slap and began to slide slowly towards the floor.

"Albertus Oak! What the hell do you think you are doing?" shouted Lorna Brimtide.

"Saving your life. You were going to be killed, you are the *one of air*. You are a witch!"

There was a blank expression on Lorna's face, and I realised that I hadn't told her anything about the séance we had conducted with the Ouija board, nor about what we had found the night we had decided to burgle her house.

"The next person to be murdered will be one of the air. That's you!" I continued.

"One of the air? Because I make scented candles?"

"Because you ride a broomstick!"

"No I don't."

"Just trust me." I mumbled.

Lorna continued to glare at me. The silence was short. Old Mrs Dobson broke it while rummaging in her capacious hand bag. "Just a minute loves, just a minute" she murmured, and pulled out a bag of mints, a hairbrush, a large mauve brooch, a packet of tissues, a crumpled piece of paper covered in runic writing and, finally, a large Edwardian pistol with a mother-of-pearl handle.

"There we go. I knew I had it somewhere," she announced, raising the pistol in both hands and pointing it at Lorna's head.

There was chaos. The old ladies screamed and ran about. Tombola and raffle prizes crashed to the ground, leaving the floor swimming in bubble-bath and sweet sherry. Someone carried out my original plan and set off the fire alarm. The blaring siren mingled with a shrill whistle.

Reverend Lucy and Felicity fled from the stage and out of the doors, almost knocking over Inspector Davies, who was returning with the struggling Geoffrey in his arms. I looked to the police officer for some assistance, but at the sight of the gun he seemed to be frozen to the floor with terror. Bella started to run towards the stage, but Mrs Dobson swung the gun onto her with unnerving intent.

"Nobody moves," said Mrs Dobson, the usual quaver in her voice replaced by an edge of hard steel.

I tried to reason with her. "Come on Mrs Dobson, your plan has failed. No one's going to eat your cream bun. It's over, just put the gun down."

The chairwoman of the Women's Institute scoffed. "The instructions didn't say I had to poison anyone, just that they must die. Shooting her will do the job just as well, only it makes a bit more mess." She said, with a glance at her pristine table cloth.

She was right. The parchment had not mentioned poisoning, nor even elf violet. I stalled for time. "But why? Why take the risk. How do you know it will work? Do you really expect to be able to open a gateway to the invisible kingdom? On a sunny day in the south of England? It doesn't seem very likely to me. What will you do when you kill Lorna and realise that nothing is going to happen? This isn't a fairy tale you know."

"Oh but it is, isn't it, Albertus? When you've lived in a village like this as long as I have you start noticing things. Weird, inexplicable occurrences seem to happen here all the time. For example, Albertus, how long have I known you? Fifty years? It has to be. And how much older have you got in that time? Barely a day. I don't think that I would be doing the first deal with the devil in these parts, not by a long shot, if you'll pardon the pun."

"I have good genes that's all," I answered. "If you do this you will not summon anyone, you will have just killed another innocent person. How would you feel about that?"

Mrs Dobson eyed Lorna. "Oh, I think I'd live," she said blithely.

"Why? Why do you want to do it? What could make it worthwhile? What will you ask for?" I questioned.

"To be young! I'll ask to be young again. I want the chance to go around another time! Do you think I want to spend my time baking cakes and hosting charity dances! I don't want to be an old lady! Being an old lady is boring! I want to go raving until dawn and sleep with boys I shouldn't! I want to make mistakes and wear fashionable clothing and travel to Ibiza for electronic-music raves. I want the beats! When I was a girl we just had to be little copies of our mothers. I married my husband at nineteen and went straight into raising a family, it's like I told you, like I've told all of you! Roast-dinners every Sunday and a trip to Bournemouth beach once a year. That's not how I want to remember my life! I want to drink jaeger-bombs and flash a policeman. I want to get into a fight outside a chip shop! I want to be sick in my handbag."

"You can still get into a fight outside a chip shop, Mrs Dobson. It's not too late," said Lorna. If she was weighing the likelihood of getting her brains blown onto the back wall then she did not let it affect her delivery.

Mrs Dobson shook her head. "It's just not the same. This is my one chance, the only wish I'll get. I won't live to see another summer solstice coincide with a full moon. Sorry love, but it's you or me."

I watched Mrs Dobson's finger tighten on the trigger, her wrinkled knuckle turning from red to white. Lorna closed her eyes.

The explosion, when it came, was not from the muzzle of the weapon, but from the huge double doors leading into the village hall. They slammed open with a crash and in bounded a dark haired dog the size of a small cow.

Bella blew her whistle again and the shrill noise I had heard with the fire alarm made sense. She pointed towards the stage. I had never seen Lupin in his wolf form before, but I had imagined him as being more wolfish. The creature galloping towards us with its tongue lolling and its ears bouncing was an overgrown St

Bernard. The old lady pivoted and dog charged. One muzzle snapped, one muzzle flashed. The room was filled with smoke. Lupin howled and twisted as the first bullet hit him.

Mrs Dobson shot again. The dog jerked but carried on. In an admirable display of sharp shooting the old lady managed to bury all six slugs into the werewolf before it barrelled into her, sending her sprawling and the gun flying to the floor behind her. Lupin carried on until he reached his goal - the remaining cream buns on the table.

Inspector Davies bravely ran forward to seize upon the prone old lady, allowing Geoffrey to slip from his arms. "I'm arresting you for attempted murder and cruelty to animals," he crowed as he slipped cuffs onto her withered wrists.

"I don't understand," mumbled Mrs Dobson. "I shot it. Why didn't it die?"

Bella spun the boson's whistle around her finger. "You said it yourself, weird things happen in this village. You should have used silver bullets."

We sat on the patio of Pentdown Hall sipping homemade elderflower champagne and enjoying the late evening sunshine. "If you think about it Geoffrey was actually quite brave coming down to warn us," said Lorna. "He must have known that if the murder was solved then he would be banished from Esmy's body and disappear forever into the unknown darkness, but he did it anyway."

"I suppose you're right," said Bella. "Maybe he wasn't that bad after all. Let's just hope for his sake there are no Moroccans in whatever place he ends up next. Do you think the fairies knew all along that Mrs Dobson was the murderer?"

"I wouldn't be surprised," replied Lorna. "Human life doesn't mean very much to them. They were curious to see what would happen and they wouldn't want to spoil their entertainment just to stop a few people dying. In the end it was lucky we had Mr Hipperty amongst them."

Lupin took a break from devouring a huge pork pie.

He always claimed he needed to eat more in the days just before and after his transformations. "Never mind if the fairies knew or not. How did you work out it was Mrs Dobson?" he asked me.

I leant back on my chair and kicked my feet onto the table, milking my moment in the sun. "It was the Bakery. Mrs Dobson was always going on about how she made all her own cakes, but before the first murder I met her coming out of Mr Fairchild's."

Lupin guffawed. "That's pretty slim evidence, Bertie."

"Well, yes, on its own it is, but when I realised how odd that one thing was, everything else fell into place. You see, on the day Geoffrey was murdered Mrs Dobson told me she had just come from Pentdown Hall. By my reasoning that would have put her there just after I had divided the elf violet and brought it up to the house, it would have been easy for her to grab a few of the leaves. She then went straight down to the bakery. Mr Hipperty said that it was the customers who persuaded him to buy a cream bun - she was one of the customers! Everyone knows that Mr Fairchild the baker keeps the best under the counter for himself, you said so yourself Lupin, so she knew which buns to spike in order to take him out next. She needed to throw those silly runes on the victim after they died so Fairchild was perfect. She could follow his ridiculously loud footfalls to whichever field he decided to stamp off to.

"That's pretty clever Bertie," said Bella.

"Wait, though, there's more. The beech tree told me someone had climbed it and watched Geoffrey die. Mrs Dobson told me that before she was married she used to love to climb trees." I was on a roll now. "She also used to be the cleaner for Sir Lionel, so no doubt she had come across both the prophesy and the recipe, and Bella gave her the number for Steve the Plumber who she invited round to look at her squeaky toilet. She gave him a bun to take away and lured him off by phoning up from a different number and reporting the leaking pipe she had sabotaged up at the old barn. She was one of the few people to have lived in the village long enough to become familiar with the supernatural, so she easily spotted Lorna for what she was, a witch, a broomstick rider, a person of the air. It really couldn't be any simpler when you think about it."

THE AFTERNOON SLID TOWARDS EVENING. We finished the elderflower champagne and old Lionel Brimtide's sloe gin. The shadows lengthened and the air became sweet with evening jasmine.

"You know," said Lorna. "A poison garden doesn't seem so appealing anymore. I think I might be getting to like roses a little more." She smiled at me and winked.

"I'll drink to that," I said lifting my glass. Bella, Lupin and Lorna raised theirs in reply. "To roses."

THE END

ABOUT THE AUTHOR

Ben Dark is an award winning writer and broadcaster based in the South of England. He specialises in working as a head gardener for eccentric individuals and he is not a dryad.

Find out more at bendark.com

ALSO BY BEN DARK

From Folding House

Coming Spring 2020

Blood is Thicker than Cider

Wittleshin is rebranding itself for the Autumn. Pumpkins are out, watercolour paintings are in.

But when bodies start appearing in the orchards the villagers suspect that someone is not ready to give up the traditions of the season.

Albertus Oak reunites his band of sleuths to clear out the bad apples and bring in the harvest. But as old feuds are uncovered and new ones set in motion it becomes clear that the past is not the only thing that haunts the village.

Coming Autumn 2020

The Dead Druids Society

Albertus Oak doesn't trust writers. Well bad luck, because Pentdown Hall is full of them. It's hosting a nature writing weekend and the star attraction is celebrity orchid-hunter Jocko Wilkinson.

But as the literati become the throat-sliterati Albertus realises that some writers are much less trustworthy than others. Only with help from his friends, and a few choice plants, will the gardening dryad discover which guest needs to be pruned.

For more information please visit bendark.com

Printed in Great Britain
by Amazon